LOVE
& HOMEGROWN
MAGIC

PATRICIA BOSSANO

WATERBEARER PRESS

Love & Homegrown Magic

Cover design and art by MiblArt

Edited by Kelsey E. Gerard

Published in the United States by WaterBearer Press
www.waterbearerpress.com

ISBN: 978-1-7325093-3-7 (hc)
ISBN: 978-1-7325093-4-4 (sc)
ISBN: 978-1-7325093-5-1 (e)

BISAC:
Adult Fiction: Religion & Spirituality, Occult & Paranormal, Supernatural, Magic Studies, New Age, Wicca, Witchcraft & Paganism, Astrology, Angels & Spirit Guides.
Literature & Fiction: Women's Fiction, Domestic Life, Sisters.
Science Fiction & Fantasy: Magical Realism, Coming of Age, Alternate History.

Library of Congress Control Number: 2020917791

WaterBearer Press Edition: October 2020

Acknowledgements

As with my previous works, *Love & Homegrown Magic* is dedicated to the Sisterhood. I could not have written this tale without your support—my cauldron runneth over!

From the bottom of my heart, Thank You, to the courageous individuals who agreed to beta-read *Love & Homegrown Magic*—I know it is a tough job and I couldn't have found a better group for the task. It takes a special someone to take time from their busy schedule to peruse unedited manuscripts and make sense out of them, so thank you: Adela, Adira, Blanca, Bobbi, Brian, Carmen, Jessica, Kelsey, Magdalena, Maggie, Kirk, Outi, Paul, Silvia, and Yanieke, you are top-shelf in my opinion and I cannot thank you enough for your candid insight and thorough critique. When you read the final version, I hope you will see your influence reflected in the pages.

It takes a village to raise a child, and it takes a tribe to produce a book. The core of mine is made up of family and friends without whose unconditional support, encouragement, supernatural artistry, and generous sponsorship I could not put pen to paper. Paul, Kelsey, Remy, Ryan, Blanca, Carmen, Silvia, and Tamra, Thank You, for being there for me with ready replies to my consultations and for continuing to believe in me. You rock!

A most radiant Thank You to my dad and my other departed dears for your continued trans-dimensional guidance in my journey.

And to you, the reader, I am overwhelmed with gratitude that you picked up this book.

I hope you will enjoy reading this philosophical fiction, inspired by a birthday present. Yes, you read that correctly, one of my birthday gifts in 2020, was an Ancestral Cleanse session. You are about to dive into what that experience triggered in my mind.

Oh, and one more thing, if you notice a chapter numbering issue, do not fret. It was on purpose.

Happy Reading!

...for stardust thou art, and unto stardust shalt thou return.

Al correo de las brujas y las brujitas.

May we live on and prosper.

A Note from the Author

I couldn't have understood my life at fifteen, although I fought anyone who dared point it out to me. I couldn't have understood my life at twenty-nine, although I bristled when someone hinted at my immaturity. I couldn't have understood my life at forty either.

It has taken five decades for a full picture to emerge along with the inkling that the bulk of my energy might have been spent on the wrong pursuit. My mind, heart and body hold the collection of experiences that shaped me. But are those experiences me? As I've supposed all along?

I don't think so. There is a lot more to me—to each of us as human beings.

Beyond personal experiences, there is genetic makeup and memory; predispositions; the say of the stars; upbringing; social connections; geographical and cultural influences; learned behaviors; and dozens of other factors that impact us daily, chipping away at our sharp edges.

I've spent over fifty years handling what life throws at me with the tools I developed, courtesy of each new experience, from kindergarten to motherhood. I have measured my success based on the ability to handle experiences, always assuming I didn't have a choice over what came my way.

That was true when I was a minor, but it shouldn't have carried into adulthood. Why didn't it occur to me to plan, and choose my battles accordingly?

Because I didn't bother to know myself, that's why!

If I am to master myself now, I need to know who I am and what I want. There is no changing how I handled the experiences that brought me to this moment, but I can look back on my life and distill the essence of my nature, once and for all.

The story you are about to read is, among other things, an exercise in ancestral cleansing, a reading of signs and a changing of my genetic memory. I might arrive at the same place I am now, but this philosophical journey will make all the difference.

The tortuous path with harsh lessons about poverty, authoritarian role models, blind faith, abuse, and distrust, can transmute through acknowledgment and forgiveness. It can become a lush garden where thorns and perfumed blossoms coexist. And because along that original path there was also immeasurable love, laughter and a deep loyalty to family, the sisterhood—that magical seedling from whence an elevated life flourishes—can thrive.

The retelling of events is akin to reliving them, it is covering the ground in someone else's shoes, and it is how understanding dawns so that harmony can be achieved.

Sweet Virgin Mary, Angels in Heaven.

Thank you for all the blessings in my life. Thank you for my mother, and my father, and all my brothers and sisters.

In your name, I pray.

Chapter

1

T he Gemini constellation paused in the heavens the afternoon Maggie was conceived.

The mischievous Twins looked down upon the lovers, Dolores and Vicente, intrigued by the opposing temperaments fused in the earthly act. Love and devotion meeting passion and overriding determination, caused every star in the constellation to glitter in complicit enjoyment of the union. But the Twins—who could see far and wide—knew something more than love was afoot.

Determined to have a hand in it, they flashed their blessing across the twilit sky, adding traits of bravery and loyalty to the ovum and seed.

Thus, began the rapid development of the star-dusted embryo.

The celestial bodies resumed their cosmic dance and swirled aloft for forty weeks, until Pisces swam in, during the rainy season, in the year of our Lord, 1939.

For days on end, torrential showers drenched the primeval farmstead, Santa Victoria, causing streams to swell and valleys to flood. Yet,

February the twenty-fourth dawned in eerie silence—neither the singing of the birds, nor the chatter of the monkeys disturbed the dewy equatorial forest.

Since her labor pains began, near one in the morning, not a drop of water had fallen from the sky.

Alone in the hut, under which half a dozen chickens scratched the mud looking for grain, lay Dolores on a lumpy mattress, on the bare floorboards. She did not cry out, not once, only the sheet crumpled in her fists denoted the merciless attack of each contraction.

Through closed eyelids, she perceived the bolt of lightning and she heard the whip-like crack of thunder. Rain breached the canopy of trees and roared over the tin roof, flushing Maggie out of her mother's womb.

Dolores' fists unfurled. Blindly, she reached for the slippery baby still connected to her. She began wiping her daughter's face with a damp rag while, with a final spasm, her uterus expelled the placenta.

A ray of misty sunlight slipped through the gaps in the bamboo walls and found Dolores, humming a made-up lullaby, with the infant at her breast. When Maggie opened her blue-yellow eyes, she gasped—never had Dolores seen such a knowing glance. It filled her with dismay for it spoke of a life already lived, with a clear and irrevocable purpose.

Before sundown, that same day, Dolores gathered her strength and buried the placenta in the back garden, as she had been taught by her own mother, God rest her soul.

From it, by and by, grew a peculiar rose bush. Undetected, for daily life at the farmstead called for hard work from sunup until dusk, a new bud bloomed into a silky white rose to mark the hour of Maggie's birth. No one noticed the two white roses that bloomed on her second birthday, nor the three that came the year after that.

Not until Maggie turned four did Dolores take her down to the garden, and together they cut the four new roses to decorate their breakfast table.

"This is your rose bush," Dolores told her, "and you'll be caring for it from now on."

Maggie stood up straighter, eager to show her mother that she was ready for responsibility. She took the *mateancho* in her small hands and followed Dolores to the wellspring to fill the hollowed-out bowl with water. That morning, Maggie also learned how to loosen the dirt around the plant and mix in the smelly manure to fertilize the soil.

She marveled at the sweet perfume of her birthday roses and puzzled over what kind of magic happened, between the roots and the buds, to change the pungent smell of the manure. Maggie's curiosity led her to take the mundane task to heart. Twice a week she went down to the garden to aerate the soil and sprinkle it with water. All the while, she talked to her rose bush, and sometimes she sang to it too, fancying that the leaves and thorns whispered their secrets back to her.

On the eve of Maggie's fifth birthday, when the commotion of the day had died down and everything had to be done by candlelight, Vicente, her father, summoned her from her spot at the dinner table.

Flustered over being singled out among her siblings, Maggie climbed out of her chair seeking her mother's eyes. Cradling her swollen belly, Dolores nodded, and Maggie went to the head of the table where he sat.

Vicente scooped her up onto his lap and startled her with his gravelly, commanding voice, "Put your hand, palm down, right here on the table."

The force with which his splayed fingers hit the surface made Maggie flinch and the dishes rattle. But she obeyed and listened fretfully as her father gave each finger a name, followed by a squeeze.

Maggie's brow furrowed; panic stricken by the sudden realization that he wanted her to repeat the names!

Sure enough, Vicente squeezed her pinkie finger and looked at her expectantly.

"One," Maggie blurted out, and then, "two, three, four, and—"

She squinted at him, forgetting for a moment what the name of her thumb was. When his eyes twinkled, she heard the word he said in his head, as clearly as if he had whispered it in her ear.

"Five," she called out and Vicente laughed, delighted.

"You will be five years old tomorrow," he declared, pressing her small hand between both of his strong paws.

Maggie nodded, bewildered.

Chapter

2

While saying her bedtime prayers, as Dolores had taught her, Maggie noticed her left hand looked the same as her right, palm to palm, which made her wonder, if her right-hand fingers had names, what about the left? Were both pinkies called 'One'? She wiggled them to prompt a reply but fell asleep before she could decipher the answer.

It wasn't until Maggie went to the garden in the morning, to cut her roses, that it occurred to her the names of her fingers might not be names at all—hadn't her father said they were 'Years Old'?

Understanding glimmered just out of reach, which frustrated Maggie something awful because even at five years old she disliked *not* knowing.

The strange sense of connection Maggie experienced that morning, on realizing her rosebush had as many roses as fingers Vicente had counted on her hand, only heightened her frustration.

"One, two, three, four, five," she recited as she cut the fragrant white roses and placed them gently on the sheet of newspaper Dolores had given her—so the thorns wouldn't prick her skin. By

15

the time she got them up to the house, Maggie couldn't tell them apart anymore and couldn't figure out which was 'Five Years Old' like her.

Five is not a name, she reflected inwardly.

Over the course of her fifth year, Dolores introduced Maggie to Six, Seven, and all the way up to Ten. The concept of numbers sank easily in Maggie's fertile mind.

So it was, that when the earth had completed another trip around the sun and Maggie went down to the garden, it was with a jolt of wonder that she counted six white roses on the bush. The fleeting vision of it, utterly weighed down by roses, on a faraway day when she turned as old as her mother, made her smile. She fancied that that many roses could surely perfume the entire garden and house— and if the breeze picked up the scent, it would infuse the whole hillside and valley! Why, everyone and everything would know it was Maggie's birthday!

Nearly a year later, about a fortnight before February the twenty-fourth, Maggie inspected her rosebush with keen interest. She had been waiting all those months to confirm her suspicion and was able to exhale, satisfied, after going over it three times—there were exactly seven buds, and there was no doubt in her mind that in ten days' time they would bloom, right on cue.

In two more years, both Maggie and her rosebush turned nine. She carried within her a secret pride in the knowledge that although eleven placentas had been buried in the garden, her own included, for Vicente and Dolores had eleven children, of which ten were alive, none had yielded such an exotic plant as Maggie's. Roses simply didn't grow in that area; Dolores had assured her.

What were ferns and begonias to Maggie's mysterious roses? And what of the placentas that hadn't even produced a nameable plant? But Maggie, whose chore was to care for the whole garden by then, would lovingly clear the weeds over the plots marked for each brother and sister. She kept her thoughts and feelings to herself and would not crow over them, although privately, Maggie rejoiced and was convinced that such a thing was a sign from nature and the universe that a near miraculous future awaited.

As she arranged the nine roses in a glass on their breakfast table, Vicente announced, "When the rainy season ends, you will be going to school."

Maggie's heart skipped a beat—her father always had a way of surprising her with new words, what did 'School' mean? Her eyes darted to her older sister, surely Clara knew what that meant, but no, Clara had as blank an expression as her.

Having finished his breakfast, Vicente left the children and their questions to Dolores—she would explain it all.

That night in her bed in the girls' common room, with a lump in her throat, Maggie thought about how quickly the rainy season would be over and that she and Clara would be leaving the only home they knew. They might not return until after her next birthday—who would be there to count her birthday roses? And what could she possibly learn in school that she didn't already know?

"I know all I need," she muttered.

Maggie knew how to live off what Santa Victoria provided, she had been taught about what fruit trees needed, she could tell when they were sick and what to do about it. She could care for a vegetable garden as easily as she could tend to the hens. They had cattle, mules, and horses. She knew where to find medicinal and poisonous plants, and she knew how to sew, and make soap. She knew her way around the kitchen and could put every drop of blood and fat from a slaughtered pig to good use; to feed the family and farm hands.

Maggie seriously doubted that those 'Nuns' Dolores kept mentioning would have anything valuable to show her.

Just as she began toying with the unthinkable possibility of protesting her parents' decision, a sly thought crept into Maggie's mind to taunt her. What if the nuns were the gatekeepers of the glamorous world she had dreamt about, away from the mountain?

As if to amplify a budding sense of doubt, Maggie remembered the time Vicente had taken her to the outpost a couple of hours horseback ride from Santa Victoria. There, pasted on the dusty bamboo walls, she had seen the faded pictures of an actual city.

Cluttered buildings, sturdier and taller than the barracks row where the farm hands lived, with glass windows and doors that opened and closed with knobs rather than latches. She had seen a square, with benches and trimmed plants, that looked like her and her siblings right after their hair had been cut and washed.

Maggie knew that in a city one could find many stores too, Vicente had said as much. And they were not like their storeroom in Santa Victoria, which only had things like hemp saddle bags, hand sickles, shucked corn, rock candy, bullets, and home-made soap—all the things needed by the farmhands—but nothing pretty or frivolous.

In the pitch-black room, hands behind her head on the pillow, Maggie detected a lighter darkness outside and knew the moon must have peeked out from behind the clouds. She stared at the sliver between the wood shutter and the window box, and to the tune of her six sisters' deep-asleep breathing, their creaking beds, and their soft snoring, Maggie indulged in visions of the big city adventure coming her way.

What wonders awaited! She might no longer have to bathe in a stream but in a proper bathroom, and with store-bought soap! Not the harsh bars made of ground *piñones* and lye—those were for washing clothes. For sure, someone else would do the washing, and someone else would kill the chickens needed for dinner!

Maggie fell asleep longing for the rainy season to hurry up and pass, youthfully unaware that a dream come true, more often than not, ended up being a bitter surprise, especially when one insisted on controlling every aspect of it.

Chapter
3

Vicente De León, a powerful figure as an individual and as an entrepreneur, often left Dolores and their children in Santa Victoria, sometimes for weeks at a time. Off he would go to negotiate the sale of his crops and cattle, to promote their cause toward accessibility, or to fight for farmers' rights in local town halls. He counted on Dolores to keep things going, and Dolores counted on their well-trained children to do their share.

It was no wonder that in Maggie's mind, her parents' relationship transcended supernatural legend. It fueled her love for them along with her respect and admiration. It also fired up her imagination with daring visions of one day becoming, herself, a perfect fusion of their most impressive qualities.

Willful Maggie dreamt of being a fearless provider and a devoted partner, with a supernatural sixth sense that would serve her, as she had seen it serve her mother.

No matter how far away the object of her concern was, Dolores learned of their distress and interceded.

One night, in the heavy darkness of their room, Maggie's bedfellow, Clara, shook her. "Wake up."

"What's happened?" Maggie said, rubbing her eyes.

"Get the others. Momma wants us in her room."

Disoriented and with her heart in her throat, Maggie got out of bed. Careful not to trip over the chamber pot, she went to Emilia's bed next to hers. Pretty soon all the sleepy girls were up and headed to Dolores' room.

Through the gaps in the shuttered window of the hall, Maggie saw the telltale signs of dawn, which soothed her somehow, but not enough to distract her from a low, eerie rumble coming at them from around the desolate hills.

An oil lamp burned dimly on the nightstand by their mother's bed. Santiago, the oldest of the three boys stood by the door, holding a shotgun. The other two were huddled together on either side of Dolores on the bed.

The seven girls filed in and took seats on the floor and on the edges of the bed. Maggie pulled her feet up onto the mattress as the intensity of the rumble increased, nearing the house. Dolores rocked from side to side, her lips moving in silent prayer.

Eyes wide with fear, Maggie picked up the thread and with a commanding glance toward each of her sisters, she bade them join their mother.

"...full of grace, the Lord is with thee..."

As the rumble transmuted into a growl, Maggie's voice rose higher than the others, believing with every fiber of her being that their

voices alone, in unison, would keep evil at bay. "… pray for us sinners, now and at the hour of our death. Hail Mary full of grace…"

The thing was beneath them. Santiago braced himself against the door frame, the girls scooted together in pairs, holding hands, or embracing one another.

"Did a bull get out of the pen?" Arabella, one of the younger girls, wondered in a squeak of a voice. Olivia shushed her with a curt shake of the head.

Dolores continued to pray, as did Maggie. The thing roared under the hut, hellbent on knocking it from its stilts. Surely, Maggie would see it if she put her eye to one of the gaps on the floorboards. But she would not look, because if she did, she would give the thing permission to materialize.

"…the Lord is with thee, blessed art though amongst women…" Maggie said, full of conviction, even while the thing beneath them stomped in a fury.

At dawn that day Maggie learned that time flies when one is happy, but it will damn near stop when one is scared. The beast rattled their house and kept up the siege for what felt like an entire rosary. Yet when she thought of it later, Maggie could not remember saying more than three Hail Marys, which meant the whole affair had lasted under five minutes.

Once the sun came up, it became harder to believe that they had confronted and cast away evil, through the sheer muscle of prayer and a shotgun at the ready.

In a tremulous voice while squeezing her mother's hand, Maggie said, "Momma, could Santiago have shot it through the floorboards?"

"A bullet can't kill a phantom. Only prayers have a chance against it, and only prayers can ward off the echo of that evil that was after one of us."

Dolores' ominous reply left Maggie to wonder, in alarm, which member of the family could warrant such a threat.

Looking out the window later that afternoon, a relieved Maggie spotted her father on his horse, coming toward the farm though at a rather slow pace.

"Papa is on his way!" she called out to the house at large. Noticing the bright coloring against his white shirt, she added gleefully, "And he's bringing red flowers!"

The expected flurry of activity ensued. Vicente must find everything just as he liked it, that he might rest after his long trip. Dolores joined Maggie at the window, to glance upon the faraway image of her husband approaching.

Alarmed, Maggie saw her mother's face drain of color.

"Go fetch him!" Dolores called down to the foreman, who stood on the porch beneath them.

Maggie saw the man put his hat back on and jump on the saddled mule at the hitching post. Dolores began barking orders, which Maggie and the rest of the children scattered to carry out, under a sudden sense of menace. Clean rags, boiled water, a bottle of alcohol, needle, and thread were quickly brought into the bedroom.

To Santiago, Dolores said, "The healer." He darted out of the room and was heard galloping away on a mule.

Infinite minutes ticked by until Maggie heard Dolores race down the steps, and then she heard the struggle of at least four people moving something heavy.

When they passed into the bedroom carrying Vicente, Maggie understood—it wasn't flowers she had seen against his white shirt, he was bleeding to death.

The image of Vicente's head, perilously hanging over his chest as if by a bony rope, would be forever burned in Maggie's mind, as would be the knowledge that someone had tried to murder her father by severing his head.

Neither her nor her siblings were allowed in the room while the adults patched him up. Later she learned that Vicente had been ambushed and viciously attacked by disgruntled landowners—neighbors who didn't agree with Vicente's progressive views.

Failing to understand that the remoteness in which they lived kept them from attaining prosperity, yet fearing Vicente's influence, they had attempted to eliminate the threat he posed to their perceived autonomy.

Always suspecting foul play, Vicente had reacted in a fraction of a second and fired two shots, which found their mark. The third villain, fearful of Vicente's swift and deadly retribution, fled the scene swinging his machete and catching him across the neck as he galloped past.

It took a few weeks for Vicente to fully recover from the brutal attack. During that time Maggie learned an invaluable lesson about contrasts. Although she would never wish such an attack to happen again, *ever*, to any of her dear family, having Vicente home, under those circumstances, had allowed them all to appreciate the side of him that wasn't the landowner, the rancher, or the speculator raising them alongside Dolores.

Thus, Maggie's reverent, sometimes fearful respect for her father, began to evolve. She, along with her sisters and brothers, positively relished the guitar player in him with his brighter-than-the-sun gaze. They glimpsed Vicente, the crooner, who had serenaded their mother and stolen her heart. He had dozens of riddles to tease his children with and they cherished every bit of wisdom he delivered in his deep raspy voice.

The newfound closeness also brought with it an understanding. Maggie couldn't help recognizing the level of sacrifice and peril involved in accumulating enough wealth to get them an education. Although filled with trepidation, she must rise to the challenge; boarding school meant there would be no commuting, not daily, not even monthly! When she left, she would be gone for the whole school year, and that was that.

When the fateful day came, nine-year-old Maggie swallowed her pain. Dolores kissed her forehead before they went down to the hitching post, and nothing else was said after that. Through the blur of unshed tears, she climbed on the horse, holding tight to a satchel containing a change of clothes, a handful of underthings, and a nightdress. She would be made to wear a uniform in school, so nothing more was needed.

Her brothers and sisters stared up at her, daunted and round-eyed, as if Maggie were leaving never to return. For a moment she felt the weight of forever—if five minutes could seem like an eternity, nine months would be unendurable!

Whistling, Vicente led the way. Browbeaten and sniffly, Clara and Maggie followed him.

As her body got used to the horse's gait, Maggie began to relax, finding solace in the cheerful tune her father continued to whistle. But when she looked back and could no longer make out Santa Victoria, a lump formed in her throat. Maggie squared her shoulders, straightened herself up on the saddle and swallowed it, knowing that Vicente would not approve of tears.

Tapping into her budding dramatic flair, Maggie embraced the perception of having been banished, determined to transfigure the sickening day's journey into an adventure of sorts. Besides, the charity of the nuns who had agreed to receive them could not be spurned, and Maggie must be a model of good behavior to avoid disappointing her parents.

The horses were to get them as far as the main road, and from there, they would take a bus the rest of the way to the city. The long ride was a first for Maggie and, as such, it qualified as something to look forward to.

Her first city turned out to be a town—Maggie's expectations were nowhere near satisfied—but she held on to the promise of that dusty photograph.

As she settled into the unfamiliar dorm, fortunately, Clara would sleep on the bed next to hers, Maggie wondered if she would ever see a city like the one pasted on the wall of that outpost, buried in her faraway hills.

Chapter
4

Several years passed in unvarying fashion—the sorry leaving of her mountain home, first to one school, and later another, closer to the ocean. There wasn't much for Maggie to cling to—elusive optimism flickered far from her grasp, and she began experiencing, in the flesh, the idiom "misery loves company." She found some comfort in the certainty that, money for the journey permitting, more of her siblings would join her.

Having to trade Santa Victoria's fragrant nights, even for the faint sound of waves carried into the dorms by the iodized breeze, was a yearly agony for Maggie. A mundane journey with a dark, bitter promise, fulfilled at the end by clusters of nuns in deceiving white habits.

Maggie did her best to compartmentalize her dread; she must tuck it away somewhere where it didn't threaten her ability to function. To survive being needled with knowledge, amid daily bouts of vengeful discipline dished out by the 'sisters,' Maggie must not give it too much thought. And to preserve her self-esteem, she must breeze through the dreary chores, whose satisfactory completion meant a lesser punishment for the inmates' sinful femininity—as if they'd had a hand in being born females.

"You will kneel on those bottle caps and say your rosary."

"You must not look at your own flesh, not even while you bathe."

"You will not waste! Every bit of thread you throw away makes up the rope that will strangle you in hell."

Why, to dwell on such cruel warnings would stop her heart from its hopeful gallop.

Maggie had never known such horrors existed, that the devil lurked wherever girls gathered, lusting after their flesh, making them do his will by tempting them to succumb to acts of vanity. That the practice of personal hygiene was the devil's most fruitful opportunity to collect souls, was to Maggie the most insidious bit of learning the nuns had instilled in them. They must be clean to avoid disease, but to deny Satan, all the boarders were required to take cold showers with a bathing garment on. No lingering on the lather and rinse process. And NO mingling with the opposite sex.

Such were the moralities fed to Maggie until her fourteenth year, which spurred a tendency to sink into dark ponderings. Was her schooling diametrically opposed to her nature? Hadn't God given her her body, heart, and mind? Was it an act of vanity to be grateful for someone's compliment of her white skin, her blue-yellow eyes, her singing voice? The nuns would surely intone a Gregorian 'yes' to this.

Yet, it didn't occur to Maggie to question it outright or reject it, instead, she set about to conforming her nature to the teachings of the 'sisters' because after all, Vicente had entrusted all his children to them with a hair-raising admonition: "I leave them with you, bottoms bared, to do with them as you see fit." That meant the nuns could

wield a cane, or any weapon of choice, on their modestly covered behinds to impart their wisdom.

At the end of every school year came a three-month sojourn back at the farmstead, which would fly by despite Maggie's attempts to slow it down. Still, she treasured waking up with Dolores, before any of her sisters, to help with breakfast, and from then on, she did her damnedest to fill each day with routine tasks to stretch out the hours.

A couple of weeks into their summer vacation, following a frightening confrontation with Vicente, Clara ran off with a man no one approved of, leaving Maggie with the title of oldest sibling.

Distressing as the sudden departure of her sister had been, Maggie felt compelled to keep her wits about her. Although delighted by the unexpected bump to eldest—because it suited her skillset and disposition—she could not ignore that Clara's behavior had been a terrible blow to Dolores and Vicente. Then and there, Maggie made up her mind; she would not ever cause such grief to her dear parents.

To be sure, bossing the younger ones was a task Maggie would relish. That Vicente and Dolores acknowledged her post and responsibility as the new oldest, lessened any nun-inflicted sense of guilt over pride, which in any case, she thought it was of the righteous variety.

Maggie doled out daily chores to tend to the garden and fetch the eggs. The wash was done on Wednesdays, so scrubbers, wringers and clothesline workers were needed along with the folding and putting away later. Maggie took on the ironing herself because she didn't

trust anyone to load the iron with burning coals and apply it to Vicente's shirts without accidentally smearing them with soot.

The sweeping and mopping of floorboards happened at the end of each day. Meals had to be planned, and extra hands in the kitchen were always needed, but with six able girls at her command, nothing was ever left undone.

No matter how much tedious work Maggie engaged in though, August loomed ever closer and so did the transfer to a new school.

The family's finances had improved in the last seven years and although the three younger girls would still attend school by the sea, Maggie, Emilia and Olivia were to make the long journey to the capital.

Reluctant excitement bubbled up inside of Maggie; could this at last be the city from the dusty photograph?

She put the thought out of her mind, to save herself another disappointment.

When the day came, a truck took them to the inter-province station. They arrived covered in dust and barely had time to freshen up before they had to board the bus.

The ascent through the mountain range up to the capital would take ten hours.

The girls squeezed together on the bench seat they had managed to secure in the middle of the bus. In the cramped space with the mingled smells of sweat, dirt and victuals, they were glad they didn't have to share the bench with anyone else. It made the indignity of traveling, not just with strangers, but with their chickens, smelly cacao beans, and even a couple of piglets, tolerable.

Fortunately, throughout the long journey passengers got off and new people came in at every stop, and this provided some distraction for the girls. The driver announced how long each stop would be, so everyone knew how much time they had to use the bathroom.

Maggie instructed her sisters to go together while she saved their seat, and when the girls returned, Maggie went by herself, as the oldest should do.

Five hours into their trip, Maggie pulled out the lunch Dolores had packed for them. She distributed the baked plantains and untied the plastic bag full of *salprieta*. Since Olivia sat in the middle, she set the bag on her lap, for easy reach.

Caking each plantain piece with the flavorful, coarse powder made of ground corn and peanuts, the girls ate in silence, savoring the last taste of home they would have in a long time. They washed it down with a soda Maggie had purchased at their last stop.

The changes in vegetation became more noticeable as they sped along. When the winding climb up the mountain range began in earnest, bringing with it a change in temperature, the three girls exchanged uncertain looks—the balmy softness of their home in the lowland tropics seemed to fade more and more with every turn.

The gusts blowing in had a dry, icy bite to them, and soon the clatter of windows closing could be heard up and down the aisle, as passengers gave up their fresh air supply.

The proximity of so many bodies and the heavy exhaust fumes seeping in from the floor of the bus threatened to overcome Maggie, *but I must be strong for Emilia and Olivia.*

Claustrophobia poked at her sanity with a shaky finger. Theirs was the last window still open—they had already been given the evil eye by neighboring passengers, but Maggie would not relent, not all the way anyway, she was liable to lose her mind if air ceased to circulate. She closed the window most of the way but left a one-inch gap through, which a furious blast cooled her anxiety.

Pale and chap-lipped, Emilia and Olivia gave her an approving nod. Maggie knew she must look the same as her sisters, what with being cooped up for nearly nine hours, the lack of moisture in the air, and the cold that seemed to inject itself into them through their very pores.

"We're about an hour away," she told her sisters, and they believed her.

Outside, portly pines and lanky eucalyptus trees contributed to a wildly different landscape than she was accustomed to. She guessed they must also give the region the alien scent she detected and that would soon saturate her clothes and even her skin.

Maggie closed her eyes and forgot about the smell of pines and eucalyptus, wearily considering the altitude sickness warnings they had been given.

There was no easing her discomfort. She held still, attempting to talk herself through a rising wave of nausea. Next to her, Emilia and Olivia stared listlessly out the window, while Maggie tried to cope with the exhaust fumes wafting about as the bus wove uphill on narrow cobblestone streets.

On their bench, Maggie and her sisters swayed and jostled in unison. She stared at the colonial buildings sneaking past outside their window and fancied the whitewashed walls and red roof tiles looked like that dusty photograph she had once seen.

The climb seemed endless until, without warning, they came to a stop. All the passengers looked their way and Maggie realized it was because they were the only school-aged people on the bus.

Following Vicente's instructions from over ten hours before, the driver ushered the three girls, with their small satchels, off the vehicle and led them to a massive adobe archway with a chained iron gate. Maggie stiffened.

On the side post of the archway there was a box, too high for any of the girls to reach. The driver opened it and rang the bell—the sound echoed back as if from a deep cavern. Maggie shuddered.

An ancient nun materialized, dressed in black, with a wooden cross strung around her neck, to unlock the gate. The key grating into the padlock, the chain clanking, filled Maggie with dread. Had the driver not spoken at that moment, she might have bolted, dragged her sisters to the bus, and demanded to be taken back home.

"This is Maggie De León, and her sisters," the driver said, in an exhausted voice.

He left them there without pomp or ceremony.

Emilia and Olivia instinctively drew closer to Maggie, whose legs were starting to shake on account of her effort to keep a firm stance.

No greeting, glance, or smile came forth from the nun. She stepped slightly to one side and Maggie understood they were to go in. She motioned for Emilia and Olivia to follow her, despite the feeling that her heart was being squeezed to a point it might stop beating.

The cloister's gate shut behind them with a mournful groan.

An entire nine months would pass before Maggie could return home for a few, meager weeks. How was she to breathe in such dismal, wintry quarters?

For Emilia and Olivia's sake, she would.

Chapter 5

ithin the scope of contrasting forces shaping her character, Maggie became a dazzling young lady on the verge of obtaining a door-opening diploma.

On the one hand, she embodied the organic splendor of the lowland tropics, replete with love, devotion, and the aggressive confidence modeled by Dolores and Vicente. While on the other, just beneath the surface, swirled currents of the unyielding, oftentimes cruel, discipline instilled in her by women, whose life experience amounted to never ending hardship and sacrifice, as demanded of them by the Vatican.

Maggie often wondered, would they die—the nuns—and find themselves in heaven, one fine day? Would choirs of angels extol their lives of self-denial? Or would they be confronted by demons in the yawning mouth of hell, asking them why they'd taken pleasure in tormenting young minds and twisting their hearts.

But like many other such thoughts, Maggie compartmentalized them deep inside, denying them any power over her. Just distant storm clouds on the horizon.

For several years, Maggie's life had been a grueling cycle of three months of refueling in Santa Victoria, followed by nine months of unrelenting compromise in school. Maggie had learned to survive by stifling her wild heart with a practical mind. When her blue-yellow eyes looked on the world, it was from the vantage point of a pawn who wished to break free from the hold others had on her.

Gone were Maggie's dusty, photographed illusions. In her dreams, she had leapt over the cloister's walls and seen herself in a world beyond her country and kin. The vision would not leave her.

Her honed ability to sock away emotions, together with the small pleasures the school boundaries allowed, gave Maggie much needed strength to plow through to graduation.

Though it was an epic feat, as mixed social events were only once a year, Maggie had developed friendships with students from the all-boy school her brothers attended. She had upward of three aspiring beaus, but one in particular had her attention. She considered him a serious threat to her heart.

"Why can't we go?" Olivia complained bitterly one afternoon, "even Sister Temperance says we can, if only you let us. Are you afraid we'll tell on you? Miss I-want-to-be-a-singing-movie-star!"

"Or is it because that Alonzo Navarro is going to be there?" Emilia chimed in with a shrewd lilt in her voice.

"I told you already," Maggie seethed, "only five girls are allowed, and all spots have already been taken up by older girls."

Maggie stared her sisters down, determined to conceal her disappointment at being read so easily. Not so much for the juvenile dream of becoming a singing sensation, but for Alonzo.

She wanted to punish her sisters for taking from her that fleeting quiver of excitement the smuggled note had given her. Couldn't they let her have that at least?

"Neither of you are going, and that's that," she snapped.

So what if the resentment they leveled at her now had been cultivated by Maggie herself? To her mind, being the eldest certainly absolved her.

"The burden of responsibility has its perks," she muttered, for guilt would *not* threaten her enjoyment of that rare, chaperoned outing older students were allowed. She had earned it.

Maggie knew that refusing permission to her sisters endeared her to the nuns, who on occasion liked to play the 'good Samaritan' with the younger girls. Coming off as the mean older sister was a fair price to pay to keep Emilia and Olivia from witnessing her interaction with Alonzo.

Harmless though it would be, Vicente was not a tolerant man when it came to the virtue of his daughters, especially after Clara's affront. Maggie could not risk having her sisters send word, particularly at present, for on the recommendation of Mother Superior, a nanny position had been secured for her, in New York City.

For three weeks, as letters came and went between her parents and Mother Superior, Maggie held the tantalizing secret in her heart, not breathing a word of it to a single soul—not even her sisters—in the certainty that the whole scheme would be jinxed if she did.

Convinced that a worthy future for their daughter awaited in a foreign land, Vicente and Dolores had already, through a great deal of sacrifice, scrounged up the money to fly their daughter to the

United States—Maggie would be first in the family to travel such a distance from home!

Tucking away the unpleasant exchange with her sisters while she got ready, Maggie steadied her mind in preparation of her encounter with Alonzo. Now her departure was certain, she had so much to tell him.

Like a prayer under her breath, Maggie said, "Let him get there early so we don't have to wait until the intermission for our first conversation!"

She dabbed her mouth with homemade lip wax, dyed with a hint of red. She flung aside the curtain divider and left the girls' dorm without a backward glance.

Chapter
6

As it happened with any of Maggie's fervent pronouncements, events aligned and came to pass accordingly. The fact that the resulting circumstance wasn't exactly as she had envisioned, helped cloud Maggie's understanding of her power.

In the theater's main hall, Maggie glanced surreptitiously in every direction hoping to find Alonzo. The two chaperones had gone into the restroom, and her four classmates were looking about excitedly—theirs was only the anticipation of an evening with the Philharmonic Orchestra performing Prokofiev's *Peter and the Wolf*.

There he was!

Their eyes met and Maggie glided toward him, excusing herself as she navigated the crowded hall. This was their fourth meeting, and Maggie was annoyed there wouldn't be a chance for them to talk at length. He had hinted at the imminent declaration of his love, but she would deliver a fatal blow to their budding courtship instead.

In deliberate fashion, Maggie held out her hand and Alonzo took it in both of his—eyes glistening with emotion.

"I am so glad you are here early," he said, a pleasing eagerness marking his words.

"Me too! I have some exciting news I must share with you," Maggie sang, although a frown immediately darkened her brow, aware of the careless choice of words—Alonzo would find her news anything but exciting.

"Looking forward to hearing it!" he assured her, oblivious to Maggie's remorse.

The chime sounded, signaling the performance was about to begin.

They hastened to exchange seating details so they could share impressions through mute glances as the production developed. They also agreed to meet in the main hall, promptly at the beginning of the intermission.

The evening transpired as planned, yet after the intermission, the climactic performance of the Philharmonic went unheard by the wounded lovers. Indeed, the Maggie who had arrived at the theater a mere four hours before was quite altered upon her return to the schoolhouse.

Maggie kept the tears in check until her curtain was drawn, and she could hear the breathing patterns of the girls sleeping in the dorm. She snuffed out the candle on the night table and settled on her creaking mattress.

He'd given her his handkerchief when he saw the tears shining in her eyes—it was the same handkerchief with which she now dabbed her eyes. She found herself chasing the subtle scent of spice still clinging to it.

Will she ever forgive herself, or forget the pain she had caused him? She rolled onto her side, stifling her sobs on the pillow as their final exchange replayed in her mind.

Pressed against the lobby wall, Alonzo had shielded her from the curious glances of patrons on their way to the lounge area, while Maggie blurted out her news.

"I've been placed with a family in New York—they need a nanny, and Mother Superior recommended me highly for the position."

Alonzo had stared at her, a disbelieving crease above his nose.

"I will leave a week after graduation," she added miserably, detesting the harsh finality of her own words, aware that they didn't allow for negotiation.

"That's less than a month away," Alonzo had stammered, taking a step back and letting a chill draft reach her—the cool air filled the space between them, slipping through layers of cloth and flesh alike.

Perhaps it had been the heightened emotion of the moment, or that he was standing so close to her. Whatever the case, Maggie realized her feelings for him ran deeper than a fleeting attraction, and she was convinced anew of Alonzo's devotion. Yet even though she had seen the heartbreak in his eyes, Maggie felt powerless to rid him of it.

In the moment, and at present, her mind overruled her heart as she coolly assessed the situation; the hardships her parents and siblings had faced, and would continue to endure, to make the trip possible; the high praise heaped on her by such an authority figure as Mother Superior; and Maggie's own far-reaching dreams, made the trip to New York impossible to abandon. She would not hold her heart, or Alonzo Navarro for that matter, above her family.

"I'm leaving, and that's all there is to it!" she sniffed onto her pillow.

There was no time for a visit to Santa Victoria before leaving the country. Instead Dolores and Vicente came to the city for the graduation ceremony, glad to be there for Maggie and to see their other six children too.

A frugal dinner, at the home of Mother Superior's brother, followed the ceremony. Afterward, the family ambled through the colonial downtown, looking in store windows and garden gates, making halfhearted remarks that—to Maggie's mind—contradicted the liveliness she had grown up in.

With a distant look in her eye, she studied the mixed sensations seeming to saturate their collective spirit. It soon dawned on her that she was projecting, onto them, her own confusion. After all, forty-eight hours hence, she, Maggie, would be the first in her family to jump on an airplane!

Such exhilaration carried with it a degree of hesitation, which bred trepidation tinted with grief over the dear people she would leave behind.

As if to save her from herself, Olivia grabbed Maggie's elbow, directing her attention back toward the handbag in a leather shop they passed.

At her sister's touch, Maggie experienced Olivia's overwhelming sense of hope, her compelling elation over the promise of change.

Unable to refuse the powerful shift, Maggie allowed grief and hesitation to leave her at once. In a bright flash, she understood and embraced her purpose; to lead the way for her siblings.

Welcoming a sudden buoyancy of spirit, she looked at the faces of her loved ones and beamed.

"That *is* beautiful!" she said to Olivia.

"You shall have it then," Vicente said gruffly.

"Can't arrive in New York without a proper handbag," Dolores smiled.

"Oh! Thank you so much!" Maggie said, hugging Dolores and then Vicente—she was to have a store-bought purse! She could see her passport already tucked in there, along with the little bit of money she had for incidentals, until she started getting paid.

Gone were whatever petty resentments Maggie and her siblings may have harbored before—the gate to the wide world had been thrown open, and Maggie would be the first to venture out there, to mark the path her family would follow. She felt more than up to the task.

From a quiet corner in her heart, Alonzo gave her a sad, hopeless smile. Maggie turned her mind from the sight.

Chapter
7

The summer of 1961 had just begun, and Maggie had to own that the most impressive appeal New York held for her was how she felt being there; invincible, on the verge of greatness.

Never mind the airports, the flights, or the impossible high-rise buildings—nothing colonial about them! Never mind the crackling multinational energy of the city, or the sweltering summer heat. Or the miracle of miracles—uninterrupted flow of electricity and water to every household, even the lowliest of citizens could count on that!

Yet, none of those first experiences or newly found comforts compared to the conviction bubbling within and sustaining her. In New York, Maggie meant to improve her English, and work diligently to have her own place, while saving money for her family to come to her.

She couldn't have dreamed up a more auspicious setting in which to begin the rest of her charmed life.

The family hosting Maggie consisted of a sullen woman, Lourdes, in her mid-thirties, currently failing to find husband number three, and her children; an awkward young man of nineteen named Julian, and Maggie's charges; a seven-year-old boy and a five-year-old girl.

As it turned out, Lourdes was not only Maggie's employer, but her landlady too. Her second husband had left her the neglected four-story apartment building, in lieu of alimony and child support. Lourdes and her offspring lived on the spacious ground floor, and their only income came from leasing the upper flats.

In an accent that was at once familiar and off-putting, for it put Maggie right back into a cell in the old schoolhouse, Lourdes explained that there were two, two-bedroom apartments on each floor. Nodding, Maggie followed her up the stairs.

"She is at work right now," Lourdes said, opening the door to Maggie's new home on the third floor, "but her name is Eleanor and you will room with her."

So, Lourdes can get in and out of this place whenever she wants, Maggie thought, unsettled, but she shook off the ugly sensation and followed her inside.

There wasn't much to take in, one side of the apartment contained a sitting room, dining area and kitchenette. Opposite those, was a hallway, at the end of which was a single bathroom.

"Yours is the one on the right," Lourdes jutted her chin toward the closed door in the middle of the hallway.

Maggie opened it and peeked inside.

Despite the worn carpet, she was delighted that the barren room had a window, never mind that the view was of the brick building across the alley. The twin bed, with matching nightstand and mirrored dresser would do fine for her meager belongings. Compared to the girls' dorm at school, this was unheard of privacy. And to think, the one bathroom would be shared only with Eleanor, what luxury!

After Maggie's arrival, the first few days passed in a blur of getting acquainted with her situation and with her roommate—within a fortnight she knew Eleanor would be like a sister to her, for their lives to come.

The more information she and Eleanor shared, the clearer it became to Maggie that she had been misled; her paycheck barely covered the amount Lourdes charged for the room. If she was going to save any money, Maggie needed to find another job.

Of course, she absolved Mother Superior; how could she know how her twice removed relation had turned out. And her parents were absolved as well for they had placed blind trust on the nun's words.

"I hate to disparage a fellow countrywoman," Eleanor said, and Maggie smirked knowing serious derision would be forthcoming. "She walks a tightrope with how much she charges us. The place barely meets municipal requirements! She's so greedy she won't pay for maintenance, and she knows we won't complain because—" Eleanor's eyes narrowed and her voice dropped to a whisper, "some of the tenants here have overstayed their visas."

Maggie leaned across their dining table causing Eleanor to lean in too. "She sent me to do the shopping twice last week," she hissed, fearful her voice might carry through the heating ducts, "and she didn't pay me for the groceries because she said that since I eat lunch with them, all four of them, it's only fair that I pay for the food, and cook it too!"

Eleanor leaned back on her chair looking enraged. "The nerve!"

Maggie nodded.

"We need to get ourselves out of here," Eleanor said drumming her fingers on the table, "and for that, we need to get you another job!"

Into the third week of the rest of her life, Maggie was fighting the feeling of being swept by a current fraught with daily, sometimes hourly, changes. She resented not having leisure time to examine them before making decisions.

In her darkened room, after saying her prayers, Maggie tried to convince herself that choices were still hers, no matter how swiftly changes cropped up.

For the first time in her life, confronted by a need to make speedy decisions, Maggie stopped saying traditional prayers like Our Fathers and Hail Marys. She felt that neither God the Father, nor his Son, should be bothered with such mundane matters as assailed her. In their stead, an entire network of archangels was at her disposal, courtesy of Dolores.

To them, Maggie began formulating her own requests, to serve her own purposes. She dispensed with the conventional in favor of her own, authentic approach. The pertinent archangel would be called upon with a fervent, "Guide me!" or a "Light the way!" and invariably, a ruling came to her overnight.

Celestial guidance resulted in Maggie enrolling in free night courses at a City College, to improve her English. She also agreed to part-time employment at the Flower Shop Eleanor had referred her to. Its flexible hours allowed Maggie to work afternoons or evenings, as needed.

But no sooner did the roommates feel they were getting ahead than Lourdes devised a way to increase their rent.

On checking their mailbox one afternoon, along with their usual stack of ads and the occasional letter, Maggie spotted the folded notice.

Livid, she raced upstairs to show it to Eleanor.

"It's like she wants us to leave!" Maggie blustered, "she wants another two dollars a week. Here." She gave Eleanor the slip of paper while, with a violent tremor, she flipped over an airmail letter from the pile—her name was written on it, in a handwriting she couldn't fail to recognize.

"I believe you're right! The woman can't hide her greed and we can't let her—"

Maggie looked up at Eleanor, shocked by how swiftly the rent issue had left her mind.

"Are you okay? The color's drained from your face!"

Astonished by the two paragraphs she'd already read; Maggie couldn't answer right away. She read the letter again.

"Yes, I'm fine," she stammered.

Maggie had already shared Alonzo's story with her roommate but was still hesitant to let Eleanor read the letter for herself.

"What is it?" Eleanor insisted, and a flustered Maggie handed her the single sheet of paper.

"He's coming over, he'll be here a week from Wednesday?"

Hearing Eleanor say it was even more shocking. Maggie nodded, unable to define her state of mind; excitement, a tender sense of devotion, and a little bit of irritation over the intrusion a visit meant, all vied for her acknowledgement. That is, until her mind conjured up his face, his loving eyes, and the sensation of his lips on her hand.

Maggie's confusion crumbled then—eleven days must pass until Alonzo came, how was she to endure it!

Chapter
8

To overcome the anxieties and setbacks of the last three weeks, Maggie hitched her positive attitude back on, figuring that only by embracing her discomforts would she be able to let them go.

She felt confident she had Lourdes' character pegged and could take her on. The two young children were sweet and, come the end of August, Maggie need only watch them after school, which opened her schedule to work more hours at the Flower Shop. As for Lourdes' older son—a useless lurking presence whose disturbing glances caused her serious mistrust—Maggie decided to simply ignore him.

She could not allow Lourdes and her family to interfere with her vision. The notion was so intense that Maggie took to repeating it, like a mantra, several times a day, "They're not a permanent fixture in my life. Soon enough, I'll be beyond their influence."

Three days before Alonzo's scheduled arrival, Maggie agreed to accompany Eleanor to meet a young man she was interested in. His name was Mario, and upon Eleanor's urging, so that there wouldn't be anything untoward about two ladies meeting one gentleman, Mario brought his roommate to complete a foursome.

"Maggie, I'd like you to meet my friend, Angelo Moretti," Mario said.

Maggie held her hand out to him, dazzled by the enthusiasm with which he took it. She held Angelo's glance, surprised at her own audacity in allowing him to construe what he would from it.

"What an unexpected pleasure!" he said, warmly shaking her hand.

In Maggie's mind danced sudden ponderings, not that she would see Alonzo in three days, but could meeting Angelo be the work of the Holy Trinity? *He is still shaking my hand—how long has it been?*

Shamed by such thoughts, the color rose to Maggie's cheeks. Her glance hardened as she withdrew her hand. "Nice to meet you."

But the perplexing moment soon passed, and Maggie could not remember a more pleasant Sunday afternoon.

Eleanor and Mario had a familiarity about them that Maggie found quite pleasing and she became secretly convinced that they were destined to be together. As for Angelo, seldom, if ever, had Maggie been exposed to such a handsome, well-bred young man. Although nine years her senior, his mannerisms and conversation hinted at a rugged, adventurous streak that roused her interest, as such qualities were quite opposite to her calculated practicality.

She had to own; Angelo intrigued her.

The afternoon turned to evening with surprising haste, and the ease with which they had covered topics of conversation gave Maggie pause.

Fearing any kind of misconception, she told Angelo at once of the imminent arrival of her beau. Although crestfallen, he wasted no time in finding a suitable path.

"Won't you allow me to see you to and from school tomorrow and Tuesday night? Some of these neighborhoods are not safe, and I can't bear the thought of you on public transportation and on foot, at night."

"That is very kind of you," Maggie nodded, "school is only on Tuesdays and Thursdays though."

Angelo looked disappointed. "And here I was hoping to see you tomorrow and the next day," he said gallantly, "but Tuesday will have to do, and I promise to make myself scarce after that, while your beau is in town."

"Again, thank you. You are very thoughtful and understanding."

Maggie did not like the humorous look she got from Eleanor when she confessed Angelo would be driving her to school, and she positively loathed the poisonous stare she got from Lourdes and her son as they watched her get in Angelo's car on Tuesday night. Maggie guessed her rent would go up by a couple of dollars a week on the assumption that she might not be using public transportation anymore.

Later that evening, as the car idled back in front of the apartment building, Angelo lamented, "So, this is it for a few days."

"Thank you so much for your kindness, not riding the subway really is life-changing," Maggie said trying to sound lighthearted despite

the unsettling sight of Lourdes, lurking behind the slightly parted curtain of her front room.

"I wish nothing but the best for you," Angelo declared and then fell silent.

Maggie knew he hadn't meant for it to sound like a last goodbye, but she couldn't think what other farewell would have been appropriate under the circumstances.

"Thank you again," she stammered, "I hope all goes well with you, until we meet again."

Angelo smiled at this, and seemingly heartened by her words he got out of the car, walked around to the passenger side, and opened the door for her. He walked her to the doorstep and warmly shook her hand before he left her.

Chapter 9

Right after her prayers that night, in a deliberate fashion, Maggie whispered to herself, "Alonzo will be here tomorrow afternoon."

She wriggled in bed, satisfied that although she'd reminded herself of it throughout the day, the looming arrival still caused her heart to beat faster. She took is as a sure sign that her feelings for Alonzo were true, at least as true as his, and would not explore beyond that.

Sitting for the kids on Wednesday quelled Maggie's anticipation of the afternoon and evening—she went through the motions of coloring and playing card games. She fixed bologna sandwiches for lunch and tidied up the kitchen afterwards. Then, deviating from her normal list of suitable crafts, and since Lourdes was away, she agreed to let them watch television.

Maggie stared dreamily at the black and white images but did not hear a word *Howdy Doody* said, instead she wondered, would Alonzo find her changed? Would he be any different? It seemed impossible that they had last met only five weeks ago! She began to appreciate how thorough the melding into a new world had been—Maggie felt she'd been in New York an entire year, at least.

Lourdes and Julian returned after the episode concluded and, while reaching for her purse on the hook by the door, Maggie reported on how well-behaved the little ones had been.

Eyeing Maggie suspiciously, Lourdes remarked, "You seem to be in a hurry."

Julian made an abrupt pause between rooms, as if curious to hear the reply.

Noting their expectant looks, Maggie hitched the purse strap on her shoulder and grabbed the doorknob.

"I'm expecting a friend—should be here presently," she said, careful to withhold the gender of her caller. "I'll see you tomorrow!" She darted out the door without giving Lourdes a chance to inquire further.

"A lot of good it will do," Eleanor snickered when Maggie told her how her escape had played out, "you know they'll take turns peeping through the window until they see who comes calling."

"So, what do we do? It's too late for us to send word to Alonzo to meet us somewhere else."

Eleanor bit her lip. "Not much we can do, besides, he will be in town for a few days, so we must resign ourselves. Lourdes is bound to deduce he's your boyfriend and all we can do is not give her a reason to question propriety."

"Right," Maggie snapped, suddenly outraged, "I am not doing anything wrong; I don't need to concern myself with Lourdes passing judgement on me, nor do—"

The harsh sound of the doorbell downstairs reached the third floor, stopping Maggie mid-sentence. Eleanor gave her a grim look.

"She must've locked the door, no doubt she is questioning him right now."

The color rose to Maggie's cheeks. "Let's go," she said, yanking her purse from the hook on her way out, "I won't give her a reason to think ill of me by making Alonzo come upstairs."

From the landing, Maggie could already see mother and son blocking Alonzo's way. Lourdes failed to notice the arrival of Maggie and Eleanor, engaged as she was in efforts to detain him with her smarmy commentary.

How Maggie resented to have this special moment tarnished by those two deplorable individuals. Who knew what kind of information they were trying to extract from Alonzo!

Before she could think what to do, Eleanor swept past Maggie, and hooked her arm to Alonzo's.

"So happy to see you!" she twittered, pulling him away from Lourdes and back toward the front door.

"Oh! Why, here she—they are," Lourdes stammered sourly as Maggie grinned and hurried after Eleanor.

On either side of a bemused Alonzo, Maggie and Eleanor broke into laughter as they pulled him along down the sidewalk.

"What was that all about?" he grinned, caught up in the levity of the situation.

By the time Maggie apprised him of the circumstances and recounted her impressions, she felt their relationship had received an influx of closeness equivalent to several months' acquaintance.

Over the next few days, their exchanges became relaxed and candid, so unlike what they had experienced back at home, where they were expected to be guarded and proper, at all times.

Since in Maggie's opinion Eleanor was not an adequate chaperone, Alonzo could not be asked to visit their apartment, instead their meetings were out of doors, and thank goodness for long summer evenings! Maggie and Alonzo walked all over town, chatting, and enjoying the sights. Eleanor would accompany them on occasion, but mostly they were on their own.

At the end of his first week there, while walking in Central Park— apparently unable to contain himself—Alonzo paused beneath an enormous elm and turned to face her. He clasped her hands in his and Maggie braced herself for a declaration.

"I love you, Maggie," he said, eyes shining with the sentiment.

Her breath caught in her throat; she couldn't think what to do so she squeezed his hands by way of a reply.

Alonzo took that as encouragement and went on, "We can marry in City Hall next week—"

Alarmed, Maggie's eyes widened, and her smile faltered. Alonzo hastily amended his proposal.

"Or I can extend my stay for a few more days, if it pleases you, and in due time we'll return home for a church wedding."

Maggie could not reply, she cast her eyes down, bewildered by the multitude of thoughts and sensations assailing her. The warm caress of the New York breeze that evening, would never be forgotten.

"Your eyes are so beautiful," he went on, brushing a lock of hair away from her face. "In them I can see the turmoil my words have caused. Share your thoughts with me," he pleaded.

The pressure mounted but Maggie would not let it overwhelm her; she must dispel the warmth his declaration had enveloped her in. *I can't afford a state of heart when a sound state of mind is what's called for*, such were her thoughts on raising her eyes to him.

"I love you dearly," she paused, detesting the notion that a 'but' should follow such a statement. She opted to expand her opener, "Next to my family, there is no one I care for more than you, which is why I know you'll understand my request to delay."

Alonzo's shoulders sagged, and Maggie felt his misery the moment her words pierced his heart. She wished she could stop, but otherworldly forces compelled her to express all the reasons for her decision.

"After all my parents went through to give me an opportunity like this one—to my mind, going back after being here for barely a month would be akin to a betrayal. I would be throwing away the future they gave me, the bid they made, without even a cursory effort on my part to make something of it. It would be like spitting on their sacrifice."

It was Alonzo's turn to look away. Dismaying seconds ticked by in silence until Maggie's grip on his hands began to relax—her fingers had begun to tingle. That seemed to wake Alonzo from his reverie, and he turned a resigned glance on her.

"I understand. And I couldn't live with myself if you acted against your filial loyalties on my account."

Tears welled in Maggie's eyes and, for a moment, confusion threatened to overwhelm her—had she expected him to insist? Had she hoped to be prevailed upon?

No!

How selfish could she be? Dolores and Vicente hadn't just given her an opportunity, they had entrusted Maggie with her siblings' prospects as well. Maggie blinked away the tears and cleared her throat.

"We will write to one another every week and remain in close contact that way for an entire year." But her hopeful proposal failed to inspire Alonzo, so she tried another tack, "Do you not feel confident your feelings for me will hold over twelve months?"

"How can you say that?" he replied, stung.

Maggie caressed his face. "One year is enough time for me to honor my family's sacrifice, and then you and I will marry."

It was a testament to how mature their relationship had become, that during the last seven days of his visit, despite the painful delay Maggie had imposed on him, they were able to go on with their exploration of the city in as cordial a manner as they could muster.

After a heart-rending goodbye, punctuated by renewed promises of constant correspondence, Maggie watched the yellow cab drive away, with Alonzo in it.

Like massive barrels rolling on a wooden floor, thunder rumbled across the sky. Maggie hugged herself, appraising the summer storm and wondering if she'd chosen wrong. Another crack of lightning, more thunder—so reminiscent a sight and sound, she half expected to hear the rain pummeling the old tin roof in Santa Victoria.

When the first raindrop struck her, she went back inside the somber apartment building. Out of the corner or her eye she caught Julian as he retreated into his mother's flat. Without acknowledging him, she walked up to the third floor and closed the door behind her. Since Eleanor was at work, she had the apartment to herself.

Maggie sat at the dinette table, in the dark, for the storm had snuffed out the sun's cheery light, in and out of doors. To the tune of the rain, Maggie saw what the rest of her life would be like; no matter how many opportunities to indulge herself the future presented, she was fated to approach them all in the same mind-over-heart manner.

Driven by a profound loyalty to family, to her blood, Maggie could not stray from her path.

Chapter

10

aggie meant to journey with Alonzo in spirit, it was the least she could do to share in the grief she had caused him.

She prepared for it as if for the Via Crucis on Good Friday, lighting a candle whose flickering warmth softened the flashes of lightning outside her window. Sitting lotus style on the bed, Maggie closed her eyes and saw him get out of the yellow cab at the airport, in the pouring rain.

He hauled his valise to the airline counter, checked it and obtained his boarding pass. She embraced him as he waited, wounded and patient, for the flight to board.

Fancying he could feel her presence, she kissed his forehead as he leaned back on his seat and closed his eyes for the flight ahead.

After a somber and rather late dinner with Eleanor—she had gone out with Mario—Maggie went to bed. She said her prayers and fell into a trance-like slumber, in and out of visions of Alonzo.

She endured with him the turbulence of the angry, weeping heavens and woke up disoriented near five in the morning.

Chapter 10

He has landed in Lima, Maggie thought.

There was no going back to sleep, yet in a manner unlike her, Maggie stayed in bed to make herself own up to the part she'd played in causing his pain. Only when she estimated that he had boarded his last connecting flight could she return to her senses and get on with her duties.

Five days passed in which Maggie went about her chores, school, and work in the flower shop, in a cursory way.

Alonzo's first letter arrived with the Saturday mail, and she collected it straight from the mailman's hand as he made his delivery. She left Eleanor chatting with him while she raced upstairs to read.

Alone in her room, after catching her breath, Maggie tore open the envelope and her vision clouded with tears as her glance flew over the beautifully written, heart-broken paragraphs.

"Lima, August 22, 1961

My cherished, Maggie;

An evil force fought to bring our aircraft down, I swear it, but only for your prayers I am sure we survived. Its fury attacked as we left New York, it did not let up while we changed planes in Miami, and it assaulted us with a vengeance as we made our way over the Caribbean. When at last we put down in Lima, those of us who were in better shape had to remain in our seats to allow airport personnel to attend to those who were worse off with motion sickness or were recovering from fits of terror.

The weather still hasn't let up. It is barely six in the morning and I've just had a shot of brandy, courtesy of Braniff, to calm my nerves. Perhaps I am still under the influence of this unexpected brush with death, but Maggie,

I can't help feeling that a meaningless existence is what waits for me, if cast out of your orbit.

I should not have left without you! But I gave you my word, and I will keep to our promise. As soon as I land at home, I will write to you and continue to do so every week.

Rest assured that the merest hint of a change of heart from you will have me on the next flight out, and at your doorstep!

Yours forever and always, Alonzo"

The written confirmation of the supernatural sharing in his ordeal, did not strike a chord with Maggie—she took her ability for granted. But that he had taken the experience as a bad omen filled her with a sense of doom she could not shake.

Maggie scribbled a hasty reply reassuring him of her devotion, and reiterating her end of the promise, which he was never to doubt. She stuffed the single sheet into an airmail envelope, addressed it, and licked three stamps on her way back down the stairs. With any luck, Eleanor and the mailman would still be discussing the weather and the perils of his route.

"He'll get this letter in a few days and he will feel better about our agreement," Maggie appeased herself, but doom circled in her thoughts, and its coming to fruition was soon written in her mind, like a self-fulfilling curse.

Chapter 11

The allotted timeframe in which Maggie expected Alonzo to receive her letter and reply to it, came and went. She realized it one night after school as she perused the mail left on the dinette table by Eleanor—again, no airmail envelope, and again, Eleanor was out with Mario.

Maggie took her shoes off and went into her room, wondering why Angelo hadn't returned to check on her. Eleanor hadn't dropped even a hint about whether he'd asked about her.

"Why should she?" Maggie muttered pulling her night things out of the dresser drawer. "Eleanor is too well-bred to push someone on me when she knows I'm engaged elsewhere."

Just like with Alonzo not insisting on their immediate union, it suddenly irked Maggie that Angelo hadn't come looking for her as soon as he knew Alonzo had left. There was no doubt in her mind that Eleanor had kept Mario apprised of the developments, and he in turn must have told Angelo. So why had Angelo not kept his promise?

The upsetting answer came to her, "Because what he promised was to make himself scarce. He is free to stay away, he might have met another girl. That's why Eleanor hasn't said anything!"

Reflecting on Angelo's lack of interest didn't keep her from writing and airmailing two more letters in two weeks. As Maggie sent off the latest correspondence, she went down the list of possible reasons why Alonzo hadn't yet replied—perhaps the new semester beginning was more challenging than he had imagined. Or it could be that postal workers had gone on strike. What if some tragedy struck his family?

Certainly, nothing could have befallen him without Maggie knowing of it in her dreams!

She spent a dreary Thursday afternoon with Lourdes' children—at least they were excited to have started school, which allowed Maggie the distraction of helping them with their homework instead of having to come up with crafts or games. For nearly three hours she'd been avoiding Julian's persistent glances and was glad when five o'clock arrived and Lourdes got home.

Astounded by the woman's nerve, Maggie gave a curt reply when asked about her *gentleman friend*.

"Don't take it to heart," Lourdes sneered, voice dripping with false concern, "Latin men—men in general—lose interest quickly. And absence *never* makes a man's heart grow fonder."

Bristling, Maggie grabbed her purse from the hook and left, refusing to dignify the woman's remark with a response.

Upstairs, Maggie got ready for school, sending urgent requests to the archangels to watch over Alonzo and demanding they let her know if something happened to him. She hitched her schoolbag on one shoulder and her purse on the other. She put on her flats to walk comfortably to the subway and locked the door on her way out.

Maggie spotted Julian loitering in the foyer by the mailboxes, looking like he had something to say. Desiring not to hear a word from him, she let her powerful dislike act like a deflecting shield, so effective as to gag him as she sped by. She could feel his eyes on her back as she swung the door open and stepped into the cooling September evening.

Leaning against his car in a dashing stance, the passenger door already open for her, Angelo smiled.

Maggie kept her response in check, at least until she could explain to herself why the pleasant surprise wasn't at odds with the mission she had entrusted to the angels. *I will marry Alonzo in eleven months, and that's that!*

"Would you like a ride to school?"

Maggie smiled without meaning to and addressed him with a warmth she hadn't allowed herself before. "Hello, Angelo. Thank you, yes."

True to her sense of integrity and loyalty, Maggie told Angelo how things had been arranged on Alonzo's departure.

"I can't discount my parents' sacrifice or dash the hopes of my siblings without a genuine effort. That's why we agreed to wait one year."

"And I will be here, to ease the strain of the wait," he offered readily.

Angelo's roguish, adventuresome streak made Maggie grin in spite of herself. But the compelling need to alleviate flyaway concerns, soon had her reasoning that his offer to 'be here' meant no disrespect to Alonzo, rather it put her in the driver seat, which was how Maggie liked it.

All she need do was set and enforce boundaries, and everything would be fine.

The autumn equinox, however, found Maggie entrenched within her boundaries, subjugating expectations, and building up the courage to start a new phase.

She had written six letters to Alonzo and he had not replied. How many more should she write? How much longer would she speculate on what became of him before she accepted that Lourdes had been right; absence had *not* made his heart grow fonder.

Meanwhile, with her usual fondness for devious exploitation, Lourdes continued to raise their weekly rent. "Some of us still ride the bus and take the subway," she jeered one windy afternoon.

A sniveling Julian handed Maggie and Eleanor their rent envelope, with a crossed out $19 and a scribbled $23.

"For ninety-two dollars a month we can find an apartment in a better neighborhood," Eleanor muttered.

"Assuming you have good credit and the money for security deposits and such," Lourdes said, certain of having the upper hand.

Maggie listened in silence, resenting her landlady for making sure they didn't have a chance to save, much less build a credit history—all their dealings were in cash.

Julian caught her eye and Maggie recoiled from the greedy look he gave her, unnerved by the impression that his greed had nothing to do with money.

Outside of Maggie's domestic turmoil, Angelo had become the breath of fresh air she counted on to whisk her away from her doubts about Alonzo, and her desire to, once and for all, in a Christ-like manner, overthrow the money changers' tables from the temple of her future.

Maggie wouldn't dream of asking for help, much less become indebted to Angelo, no matter how honorable and gentlemanly he was. No, Maggie must do the best she could on her own. Nevertheless, she was grateful that Eleanor often regaled Mario and Angelo with stories of the dreadful Lourdes.

Unable to prevent it, Maggie secretly rejoiced in that the two gentlemen were as outraged as they.

The merciless October wind blew all the leaves from the trees. No longer was the city ablaze with fall colors, instead, the naked branches seemed to clamor to the sky, "Clothe me!"

On a Sunday morning, as she stared at the brick wall outside her window, Maggie considered herself in similar fashion.

She was in her bed; under a thin blanket she'd pulled up to her chin to guard from the cold. On top of the nightstand, sagging from wear, sat the leather purse her parents had purchased over four months before; inside the dresser were the same under things and clothes she'd brought from home.

There was nothing new inside her purse, or in her drawers. There was no hidden cash anywhere for she had not been able to save any. Despite notebooks full of calculations, Maggie hadn't figured out how to stretch her minimum wages at the flower shop, or the few cents Lourdes reluctantly parted with every afternoon.

A passing cloud covered the early morning light, adding to Maggie's glum mood. She rolled over on her side and swallowed the knot in her throat. A thicker blanket, a heavy coat, a pair of boots for winter,

a savings account, these were all things Maggie thought she would have by now. There should have been at least eight letters from Alonzo by now too, for her to find solace in rereading.

The tears came forth and she indulged in a good cry until she heard Eleanor stirring across the hall.

With a heavy heart, Maggie admonished herself—*sulking and regretting doesn't change things*. With that thought in mind, which she'd heard in Vicente's voice, Maggie got out of bed determined to own her circumstances and affect change.

Ready for mass, she and Eleanor made their way downstairs. They saw Julian standing by the storm door as if ready to go out himself.

"Morning," said Maggie and Eleanor in unison, eager to get past him with as little interaction as possible.

"Maggie," he spluttered, stepping between her and the door, "may I see you to church?"

Maggie had only recently found out, at the flower shop, about Halloween and trick-or-treat. For one bewildered instant, and as they were in the second half of October, she wondered what sort of trick Julian was up to, because his request certainly wasn't a treat—so said a bell, signaling alarm with a loud clang in her head.

"Thank you, no." Maggie replied curtly, glowering at him as Eleanor pulled her out the door in lockstep.

Chapter

12

Sweet Virgin Mary, Angels in Heaven, Holy Trinity.

Thank you for all the blessings in my life,
most importantly, my family.
Thank you for your daily guidance and inspiration,
I would be lost without it.

In your name, I pray.

Chapter

12

As soon as the reading of the gospel ended and the sermon began, Maggie invoked the guidance of archangel Raphael—a crafty way of releasing herself from the dreary homily, to give free rein to her troubled thoughts.

Over the next forty minutes, hands clasped on her lap, eyes closed in deep meditation, Maggie pondered the ways she could improve her situation.

Time flew and the 'Let us pray' resonated from the pulpit all too quickly, waking her as if from a restless dream. Maggie rose to her feet and said the Nicene Creed, under her breath and in Spanish, while boiling down her reflections to three important decisions: *I won't write anymore letters to Alonzo. I will replace school with more hours at the flower shop because, as of today, my number one priority is to find a new place to live.*

Maggie crossed herself absently as the Offertory prayers were said. When the time came, she stood in the slow-moving line for Communion—lips barely moving as she whispered the Act of Contrition. She returned to the pew, careful not to swallow the Body of Christ right away; she meant to take advantage of His presence, it couldn't hurt to have her intentions sanctioned by the Son of God himself.

Maggie knelt, closed her eyes, and after a deep breath, she began repeating her three priorities in rhythmic, fervent pulsations as the communion wafer dissolved in her mouth. So absorbed was she in her thoughts and the drawn-out process of swallowing that she didn't rise from the kneeler through the entire concluding rite.

Not until Eleanor put her hand on Maggie's shoulder, did she come to, and automatically blurted 'Thanks be to God' with the rest of the congregation. They shuffled out of the church with the heavily bundled crowd, into the bright morning.

The sunlight glinting from a windshield across the street drew Maggie's glance toward an angular and handsome young man. There stood Angelo, leaning against his car in animated conversation with Mario.

Maggie's heart tripped mid-gallop.

Dazzled by the swiftness of the universe, mind racing to decipher if Angelo showing up disrupted or fit with her newly avowed intentions, she joined Eleanor in waving gaily at them.

Eleanor had said nothing about expecting to see Mario after church, so their timely presence *had* to be celestial intervention! With her doubts soothed and her faith in Jesus and the archangel Raphael reinforced, Maggie tacked on a whispered 'Thank you, sweet virgin Mary' for good measure. It was as if her decision to stop writing to Alonzo had been delivered to Angelo, at the same time she had formulated it.

Confidence blazed in Maggie's blue-yellow eyes as she greeted Mario and after a deliberate pause, Angelo. An understanding passed between them, and his entire bearing seemed to relax in the knowledge that, as of that moment, his path to Maggie's heart was clear.

Standing around Angelo's car they decided that a sightseeing tour was in order, and the discussion of where they should go was soon settled.

"I want you to see the Atlantic Ocean, with me, for the first time," Angelo said to Maggie.

Ignoring the knowing glance shared by Eleanor and Mario, she accepted with a ripple of delight.

They arrived at Coney Island and Maggie, who thus far had only seen the Pacific Ocean a couple of times in her life, stared at the angry sea creased with foam, and deemed it hostile.

"Oh, my goodness!" she exclaimed, climbing out of the car to a disconcerting sight: boarded up shops, a few stragglers braving the wind on the boardwalk, a fearsome rollercoaster, whose slopes seemed to rise up to the very sky, and the blowing sand, blurring the vast expanse between the boardwalk and surf.

"It's quite different in the summer," Angelo assured her, "we'll have to come back then, I know you will love riding the Cyclone!"

"Not on your life!" Maggie declared, eyeing the rollercoaster with dread—her stomach somersaulting at the mere thought.

They found an open café and ordered hot chocolate. Angelo put his sport coat around Maggie's shoulders as the foursome sat on a bench. They drank their beverage slowly, mesmerized by the angry pewter flashes frosting the slate blue water.

"Do you really mean it, that just two months ago this place was overcrowded with sun-bathers?" Maggie said through chattering teeth.

"Crazy, isn't it? And in the heat of August, it's impossible to even imagine wearing anything more than swimming trunks," Angelo said to nods from Eleanor and Mario.

"So extreme!" Maggie remarked, thinking of the rainy and dry seasons back at home, where there were only two settings, and neither was ever unexpected. "Do you have a favorite season?"

"For me, the end of Spring and the beginning of Summer. That's the best, temperature-wise," Angelo replied without hesitation.

"Mid-April through Mid-July, Sprimmer," Mario agreed, and they all laughed at the made-up word.

"Will it get much colder than this as winter comes?" Maggie wondered.

Eleanor winced, "Bitterly cold."

Maggie frowned, she had experienced cold within the stone walls of the girls' dormitory at school, but *bitter* cold, there was nothing she could equate that to. She would have to wait until she experienced it for herself. Maggie drew Angelo's jacket tighter around her body, promising to go to the second-hand store and buy herself a coat as soon as possible.

October's buildup to its last day, Halloween, was quite a novel experience. With a mixture of mirth and disconcert, Maggie went about her duties, shaking her head at the practices of the season.

Her sisters at home would never believe it; witches on brooms hanging from ceiling fans, mobiles hung with moaning ghosts, and pumpkins grinning toothily from storefronts. Was it against religion to participate or enjoy such things?

Maggie couldn't see the harm in it.

On a less whimsical note, she had requested, and been approved for, additional hours at the flower shop, and she soon purchased a newish, forest-green polyester coat. Maggie hand washed it to get rid of an annoying, lingering scent, and hung it from the shower curtain rod. It took four days for it to fully dry, but when she was finally able to wear it, Maggie was pleased that not the slightest chill could penetrate the synthetic quilted fabric.

Maggie wanted to quit the hours she worked for Lourdes altogether, but after discussing it with Eleanor, they decided it would be best not to, because Lourdes would certainly increase their rent then.

They let her think Maggie was still going to school, rather than working more hours, and socking away money. Falling prey to the whimsy of the season, Maggie began to dream about the day she and Eleanor could spring the news on Lourdes, the evil witch, that they were leaving!

Two days before Halloween, Maggie was hard at work making costumes for Lourdes' kids and keeping up civil conversation. Julian lurked in the adjacent room, gawking every few seconds and catching Maggie's eye. After the third time it happened, she pointedly turned her chair to erase him from her peripheral vision.

"You'll take the kids trick-or-treating day after tomorrow," Lourdes said, shocking Maggie with the unexpected demand. "I have a meeting at the city office, but Julian can go with you."

Although fuming, Maggie kept her wits about her. A chill crept up her back and she realized Julian was standing right behind her, blocking the beam of sunlight that had been warming her.

How could Lourdes impose on her like this and treat her as if she were at her disposal!

"I'm sorry, I can't, there is a program at school I am committed to," Maggie said, her cheeks flushing over the lie as much as over being treated so ill.

Lourdes blinked, and Julian came around to stand beside his mother. "And when where you going to tell me about this?"

Maggie couldn't believe what was happening, she looked from Lourdes to Julian, "I don't see why I have to inform you about what I'm doing on the weekend."

"I told you about the meeting, it was plain to me you understood I was expecting you to watch the kids on Saturday and take them trick-or-treating."

Maggie cut the thread and stuck the needle on the pin cushion. She folded the felt pumpkin she had just finished stitching and set it on the table.

"It's plain to me we have a misunderstanding. I am not available on Saturday, but the good news is Julian is perfectly capable of handling the outing by himself." Maggie uttered the last leveling a contemptuous glance at Julian. He in turn gaped at his mother reproachfully.

"This is quite disappointing, Maggie," Lourdes sniffed, "after everything we have done for you, can you not spare even two hours of your time?"

Julian gave Maggie a triumphant look that seemed to say, how will you wiggle out of that?

"I am grateful to you in the same way, I know, you are grateful for the service I provide and the rent I pay. I have no control over your expectations, or how you come by them. The fact remains, I'm committed elsewhere on Saturday."

Julian slammed his fist on the table. The radical departure from his usual clumsy solicitous self, made Maggie jump. There was that thwarted greedy look on his face again.

"Selfish, stubborn girl!" Lourdes lashed out, "you'll learn soon enough it won't do to snub us. Out of the kindness of our hearts we tried to welcome you, but you think you're just too good for the likes of us, isn't that right?"

Maggie rose from her chair, *what in the world has gotten into this woman!* she wondered, aghast. Overcome with a sudden desire to be out of their presence, she challenged, "For the life of me, I don't know what you mean, and I don't care for your insinuations or threats." She grabbed her purse from the hook and gripped the door handle, just as Lourdes rejoined.

"I better not find out your plans are with that Angelo..."

Eyes flashing, Maggie whirled, ready to speak poison, but she bit her lip and allowed herself a calming breath before saying, "You are not a parent to me, and I am not obligated to you in any way I haven't already paid for. We are even."

Julian worked his jaw as if he would say something, but it came to naught. Maggie turned her back on them and walked out. As she closed the door behind her, she heard Lourdes call out, "Not by a long shot."

Chapter

13

T he restrain displayed downstairs was forgotten in the retelling of the exchange to Eleanor.

"Goodness, Maggie, the nerve of that woman! You know what I think?" Eleanor huffed, not giving Maggie a chance to interject, "I think that awful Julian wants to go out with you, and Lourdes, being the horrible fixer that she is, has been trying to set you up with her son ever since you got here!"

Maggie nodded, "You may be right, but good grief, if that has been her intention all along, shouldn't she have—"

"Groveled more? Try to ingratiate herself? Cozy up to you?"

"Be nicer, I guess, instead of taking advantage at every opportunity and making herself so unpleasant!"

"Clearly, her greed and her maternal instinct are at odds—" After a moment's pause, Eleanor rolled her eyes and sighed, "Who knows, maybe her greed is all that matters. She's probably been trying to figure out how to get you for him, without sacrificing income."

Maggie hugged herself and shivered in the cold living room. "As I was leaving, she said, we're not even, not by a long shot. Do you think she knows I'm making more money?"

Eleanor shook her head. "In her stingy mind, she is counting on you marrying Julian, living with them, and dumping your income in her coffers. And, of course, she gets to rent your room up here to someone else!"

Maggie's jaw dropped, "We need to get out of here as soon as possible!"

Eleanor leaned in, with the air of a fortune-teller at a carnival, "You mark my words; she won't waste any time getting to Angelo, because I'm sure she sees him as interfering with her goals."

Something quickened in Maggie at the prediction, something to do with Alonzo—but what could Lourdes possibly have done about him? His visit had been so short, and they'd barely even been introduced! She shook off the thought and instead repeated her intent, "We need to leave."

The forty-eight hours leading up to Halloween became intolerable. Lourdes and Julian turned into a martial tag team; they patrolled the foyer during mail delivery, raced out of their flat when the public phone or the doorbell rang, or when steps were detected on the staircase. No doubt, Lourdes meant to get even with her, but had cunningly left the *how* of it to Maggie's imagination.

Feeling persecuted, Maggie dashed into the apartment on Saturday afternoon and threw a large paper bag on the dining table. She proceeded to take her coat off and hung it by the door while addressing Eleanor, "I hope neither of them is here tonight when Angelo picks us up for the Halloween party."

Eleanor was washing off a mud mask, careful not to wet her hair set in curlers. "Well, she's supposed to go to her meeting, and as for the little kids, they usually go trick-or-treating by dusk. With any luck, we'll miss the lot of them."

"I sure hope so," Maggie said, pulling the contents out of the bag, dazzled anew by the spray of golden stars on the emerald, velvet robe. It didn't even matter that it was second-hand because it matched the gold buckle on the witch's hat!

"Oooh! That's perfect!" cried Eleanor, ogling the set, "and you'll be nice and warm with your black stirrup pants and pullover—that's what you'll wear underneath, right?"

"Exactly!"

"You'll make a beautiful green witch."

"I'm bringing our broom!" Maggie laughed—in her mind danced images of a magical flight, side-saddle, through the lush jungles and hills around Santa Victoria.

Not having money to spend on frivolous concerns, besides lip balm, Maggie didn't wear any makeup, but for this occasion, Eleanor convinced her to deviate from the norm. "It's Halloween, for heaven sake!"

After a quick shower, Maggie sat at the dining room table, in her robe, while Eleanor rolled up her sleeves and dipped into her bag of tricks.

Maggie felt the cool tingle of wet eyeliner first, then the eye-shadow and thick mascara clinging to her lashes. A feathery dusting of rouge on her cheeks came next, and at the very end, lip liner and lipstick.

So what if Eleanor was applying the makeup on too generously? Maggie kept quiet about it. But she did tell herself, rather sternly, that she wasn't being evil. True, she hadn't seen herself yet, but Maggie was certain Eleanor wouldn't have turned her into the painted whore of Babylon. She heard that last in the voice of Mother Superior and shuddered, feeling both guilty and repulsed by the idea.

"Are you ready for this?" Eleanor sang, and Maggie felt her leaning back, as if to admire her workmanship.

"Yes!" she cried, her excitement faltering with the unexpected effort needed to unstick her eyelashes. Her eyelids too felt weighed down, but she managed it in the end, and after blinking a few times, Maggie reached for the mirror Eleanor held out to her.

She couldn't believe it; a waxy though exotic face stared back at her from the looking glass. Bit by bit, Maggie puzzled out what had been done; the foundation was a couple of shades warmer than her natural fair complexion, the black eyeliner had indeed been applied liberally, making her eyes leap out in a tropical green flash. Most shocking of all were the lips—they were not red or pink as she had assumed, instead, Eleanor had made them glittery gold to match her cheeks—no rouge had been applied after all!

"Oh, my goodness," Maggie gasped, "I look—you turned me into Cleopatra!"

"Didn't you know she was a witch?" Eleanor laughed good-naturedly, "you will look stunning in your costume!"

"Oh, my goodness..." Maggie repeated, unable to stop staring at herself, "thank you so much, Eleanor!"

She knew who she was under all the makeup, but that didn't keep Maggie from letting the enthralling effect wash over her, time and again, musing that the reality of mundane things, like emulsions, powder, and wax could expose a possible side of herself she hadn't known existed.

But really, an Egyptian green witch?

To disrupt her amusing ruminations, an overheard conversation in the flower shop flitted into Maggie's mind. The customers had alluded to an elemental wisdom contained in the pagan feast she'd heard called, *Samhain*. And again, Mother Superior hissed in her ear, "Guising is the deceiver's instrument, doomed to be trampled by the Light."

Did wearing a costume play into the deceiver's hands? The green witch in the looking glass winked, and a voice Maggie would not recognize for three decades, argued, "All Hallows wisdom is older than even Mother Superior's faith."

Chapter
14

Inhaling poise back unto herself, Maggie shrugged off disquieting thoughts about the devil and his ways—she looked in the mirror one last time and un-furrowed her brow.

Although she would never say it out loud, Maggie knew her parents' existence was, for the most part, a pagan one. Maggie's own existence would have been the same, if not for the Catholic schooling.

Dolores had raised them praying with equal reverence, to the Virgin Mary, to the angels, to the sun, the moon, and the stars. Everyone and everything had their purpose and area of expertise when beseeched. Mary, the mother of God, for matters of life and death. The angels, for mundane struggles. And the heavenly bodies, why they brought the rains and made the land bear fruit!

To the lot of them, propped on the altar of her mind and heart, Maggie had pledged her undying faith. Until the nuns came, exerting their insidious authority over her, and although Maggie respected them, as directed by Vicente, she had never taken their instruction as coming from a sole fountain of wisdom. How could she? Her life had begun and developed in ancient Mother Nature's bosom. But the dead weight of guilt instilled by the church could not be ignored, and it established levels of reverence where there had been none.

Maggie could not remember when it began, she only knew that Mary and the angels ranked above the others when she invoked them, lest her prayers went astray, or heaven forbid, were answered by something dark.

How curious, that in a flower shop in New York, Maggie had glimpsed the tip of a wisdom she could relate to more than what had been grilled into her with endless rosaries and a constant state of atonement.

What if the only purpose of Catholic practices had been precisely to squelch her more natural state of being?

Maggie's deep thoughts came to an abrupt halt as Eleanor stepped out of her room. Standing between the kitchenette and dining room with her hand on her hip, she demanded, "Well?"

"Oooooh! I can't believe it!" Maggie cried out, flabbergasted by the life-sized Raggedy Ann before her. "You have jumped right out of the pages of the book, complete with red yarn hair and triangle nose!"

"Of course, Mario will be Andy," Eleanor smiled, fluffing her apron, "did Angelo ever say what he'd be dressing up as?"

"King Brian from *Darby O'Gill and the Little People*." Maggie hadn't seen the movie, only the few posters still lingering from its release at the beginning of summer. Her smile broadened, "Come to think of it, we'll both be wearing green!"

"A pair of mismatched creatures," Eleanor remarked, with a tilt of her head, "but of the same fairytale variety, and a couple, nevertheless."

Maggie frowned. *Mismatched*, she didn't care for that word and more importantly, she didn't feel it described Angelo and her at all! She nodded absently while the frown deepened; how long had she been thinking of Angelo and herself as a couple?

"Let's go wait for them downstairs," Maggie said, gathering the emerald robe tight around herself and grabbing her old purse from the hook.

"Good idea. With any luck, Julian and the kids are gone and I'm sure Lourdes won't be back until much later."

At the landing Maggie could already tell the foyer was deserted, she reached the main floor with an added spring in her step. Side by side, Maggie and Eleanor peered out, expecting to see Angelo's car pull up at any moment.

The gentlemen did not keep them waiting long. They hurried out to the sidewalk to meet them.

Angelo's eyes traveled over the apparition that was Maggie, and she felt duly flattered despite his hilarious costume.

He tipped his leprechaun crown and performed a silly jig, drawing attention to his white socks and buckled shoes, and finished it with a flourish and a deep bow.

The evening's tone had been set, and the hilarity continued until near midnight, when the gentlemen brought them back home.

The car idled on the curb, and Maggie's belly did an unpleasant somersault on spying the hastily shut curtains in Lourdes' front room.

"Here we go," muttered Eleanor, arching her brows when Maggie glanced at her.

"Just say the word, and away we go again!" Angelo sang, oblivious to what had passed between the ladies, but his high spirits soon deflated, on seeing Maggie's worried expression.

"She's still giving you trouble then?" Mario asked.

"Worse than ever!" Eleanor griped. Maggie didn't stop her when she went on to relay the latest exchange, in which Lourdes had threatened unspecified revenge.

The knowing glance exchanged by Angelo and Mario didn't go unnoticed. "What?" Maggie implored, "has Lourdes already said something to you?"

"About a week ago," Angelo nodded, "she was on the sidewalk when I came to pick you up."

Maggie stiffened; microscopic darts seemed to prick her skin as she braced for the revelation.

Angelo addressed his remarks to Maggie, his steady glance reassuring her that he had not believed a word of what Lourdes told him.

"I won't repeat the specifics, suffice it to say she hinted that you were sent to New York by a desperate family who didn't know how else to deal with your—grave indiscretions at school."

Maggie blanched.

"Of all the slanderous, toxic, lowlife—" Eleanor sprung into a rage, but Maggie withdrew into her thoughts and didn't hear any more of the expletives.

She could not comprehend why she had been the target of such villainous libel, *grave indiscretions*! Mortified by the foul things

Lourdes might have fabricated to dissuade Angelo from courting her, Maggie averted her eyes and blinked away the tears. It occurred to her the makeup might be running now.

The green witch is undone, she thought ruefully.

At that dispiriting instant, a bright understanding came to her rescue and to set her straight. She saw Dolores, whispering prayers over her swollen womb, infusing Maggie's blood with a spell she would later compound by example.

As modeled by her mother, Maggie had learned to place equal value on physical virtue, integrity, modesty, and morality. And that meant that the desecration of one affected all.

Every instinct in her revolted. She pressed her lips together until they tingled with pain. How she wished she could leave Lourdes' unbearable dwelling at that moment, never to set foot there again!

The light touch of Angelo's fingers on her shoulder startled Maggie out of her troubled thoughts.

"I agree that you need to leave here as soon as possible," he said, and Eleanor and Mario seconded the statement.

"We're not ready," Maggie replied somberly, "we haven't saved nearly enough."

"There is an apartment near where we live," Mario interjected, "rent is pretty much what you're paying here, and it's available now."

"And Mario and I are happy to put in the deposit and first month, to help both of you get out of here," Angelo vowed.

"Good heavens!" Maggie exclaimed. Her eyes darted to Eleanor, hoping for a hint as to what should be done, "I don't know, I—"

"Maggie, we'll pay them back! Just think, we could be out of here by Wednesday! We never signed a contract, so we owe her no notice." Eleanor pointed out.

"How can it be proper?" Maggie said, hoping to keep desperation out of her voice, "Angelo, how can I accept?"

"No one has to know about the deposit, or the first month's rent," Angelo returned, taking her hand in his, "and when they see us loading yours and Eleanor' belongings into my car, you will say *your fiancé* is helping you move."

The lump formed so fast in Maggie's throat that she couldn't reply. Thoughts of Snow White, choking on Queen Lourdes' poisoned apple swam in her mind. She squeezed Angelo's hand.

"Will you marry me?"

A furtive smile played on Maggie's lips, marveling at how readily the answer came to her, now the question had been asked—*and on All Saints' Day!* A bona fide heavenly endorsement.

Without qualm or hesitation, she said, "Yes."

From the back seat, Eleanor reached over to embrace Maggie as best as she could. Mario clapped Angelo's shoulder, "Congratulations, my friend!"

Chapter
15

Caught up in a favorable autumn breeze, the foursome radiated joy; Mario proposed to Eleanor, and she accepted.

Angelo secured the new apartment on the ladies' behalf and obtained the key. It ended up not being practical to 'be gone by Wednesday' as Eleanor had hoped, so the two-week waiting period began.

The time did not go idly by. They visited second-hand stores to scope out suitable furnishings, and as funds permitted, they picked out a dinette set, a couch, lamps, beds, and kitchen utensils, which Angelo and Mario cheerfully delivered to the new place.

Time seemed to evaporate, as their excitement mounted. Eleanor couldn't even spare a moment to rub their departure in Lourdes' face, and Maggie figured they were of the same mind on that subject; both too happy to purposely dim their mood with negativity.

On moving day, it didn't take much effort to pack up their meager belongings. Angelo and Mario completed it in two trips while Maggie and Eleanor did a meticulous job of cleaning the apartment, lest Lourdes get it into her head to dock them for something.

Ready to leave the building for the last time, Eleanor knocked on Lourdes' door. When she answered, it was Maggie who spoke.

"We have the keys ready for you, just as soon as you inspect the vacant apartment."

"Julian can go upstairs with you," Lourdes snapped, eyeing them coldly over the top of her spectacles. "Julian!" she called, holding Maggie's gaze.

He came into view, wiping wet hands on his pants, and looking inquisitively at his mother.

"Go upstairs with them and make sure the apartment is in the same condition as when we gave it to them."

Julian mumbled his assent and headed upstairs. Maggie and Eleanor followed him. He took all of five minutes to look in the empty bedrooms, at the stripped beds, the scrubbed floors, the bare walls with no nail holes or chipped paint, and the sanitized kitchen and bathroom.

"Looks good," he grunted, catching a glint of the dainty gold band on Maggie's ring finger.

Let him look, Maggie thought—she had no reason to hide it.

"Then, we're done here," Eleanor said, grabbing Maggie by the elbow and making a beeline for the door.

When they reached the foyer, Maggie handed Julian the set of keys and with a terse 'goodbye' she walked out of the dingy building.

"Don't be a stranger!"

Maggie whirled and stared, unnerved by the sneer on Lourdes' face as she waved them off—*Don't be a stranger? She can't be serious!* Maggie

frowned, unable to discount the ominous suspicion that the woman might, even now, have something up her sleeve.

Julian stood at his mother's side, looking as glum and awkward as ever.

Ignoring them, Maggie turned her attention to the little ones, whose faces she could see in the parlor window—what would become of them among such relations? But it was hardly her place to address that question, and besides, she could recall a handful of occasions in which Maggie had seen Lourdes act motherly. That would have to be comfort enough to dispel any concerns over them.

She blew a kiss their way and climbed into the waiting car. Angelo shut the door after her and sprinted to the driver side. Eleanor and Mario were already in the back seat.

The new two-bedroom apartment was halfway below street level, but it faced west, which meant the sun shone through all their windows, giving it a cheery atmosphere in the afternoon. Maggie walked in, noticing an improvement in their lodgings right away, realizing it was so because Lourdes' dark aura couldn't reach them there.

"I hope you ladies like where we placed everything," Angelo said, "but if you don't, we're here to move it all around until everything is where you want it."

"That's right, because I have heard a lot about this Thanksgiving holiday coming up, and we're having it here this year!" Maggie declared, gazing fondly at her new surroundings.

"Well then, we have a whole week to prepare—do you know how to cook a turkey?" Eleanor wondered.

Maggie assented and the afternoon was spent arranging furniture, lining cabinets, and making a list of side dishes for the upcoming feast.

"Maybe we should do a potluck," Mario suggested in between tasks.

Maggie had never heard the term and as soon as Eleanor explained it, she rejected the idea, "It's not right to have guests at your home and ask them to cook!"

In the end, and in consideration of their finances, Maggie came around to it and consented to let the gentlemen bring beverages and dessert.

The outlook, the connections, the prospects, all gave Maggie the sense of wellbeing she had dreamed of on leaving her native country. She set out to dismiss the months spent under Lourdes' watchful eye as the unfortunate mishap they had been.

Chapter
16

Lounging on the couch, in her flannel nightgown, a sleepy Eleanor said, "Can you believe it? The first day of 1962 is already here!"

"Time does seem to be flying," Maggie remarked from the kitchen, where she was boiling water for coffee. Despite it being near ten in the morning, neither the overcast world outside the window, nor the frost lingering on the sidewalk could touch the snug warmth of her home.

"What a wonderful time we had last night," Eleanor yawned and stretched until her joints creaked.

Maggie nodded, "I'd never been to an actual New Year's Eve party. The most we ever did back home, besides a festive meal, was gather round my father while he played the guitar and sang."

"I tell you; my feet are killing me from all the dancing," Eleanor groaned, curling her toes.

"I did have a fantastic time too, what fun people—everyone! Maybe one day Angelo and I will have a big enough house where we can have our own holiday parties," Maggie smiled dreamily, already figuring how she might improve on the gathering the night before. "Thanksgiving, Christmas, New Year, all of it, we'll have fabulous parties, with lots of guests every time!"

"Amen to that—Mario and I will be there for sure!" Sitting up and looking over the couch's back, Eleanor added, "Speaking of fabulous parties—what'll we do about your wedding?"

"Hold that thought," Maggie said, setting a tray with cups, coffee, cream, and sugar on the dining table, "coffee's ready."

Eleanor joined her, grabbing a packet of crackers from the cupboard on the way, to complete their simple New Year's breakfast.

Sipping her hot coffee, Maggie rejoined, "We can't afford to do anything big, and it would hardly be a celebration when my parents can't be here."

She had written to Vicente and Dolores within the week after Angelo proposed. Their reply arrived in the middle of December, during the first snowstorm Maggie had ever experienced.

Holding back tears, she read their letter, realizing she'd been wishing her mother and father would somehow turn up for the occasion. Instead, the slanted words written in blue ink, spelled out her disappointed hopes; they trusted her judgement, always, and were deeply sorry they would not be able to attend.

How Maggie wished she had the means to ease their financial burden.

So, it came to pass that Maggie and Angelo joined their lives in holy matrimony, on the twentieth of January, in the year of our Lord,

1962. Following the church ceremony, a handful of their friends attended the small reception at the community center.

Angelo came to live with Maggie, and Eleanor stayed with them for the few weeks until her own wedding in the Spring, after which, she went to live with Mario.

Their happily ever after began in a golden cloud of pragmatic bliss. The couple reveled in frugality, they loaded their hearts and minds with experiences they could afford, keeping their focus on what they had promised to achieve, a big home and a thriving family.

Hand in hand, Maggie and Angelo discovered and claimed their favorite spots in the city, on foot. They drove wherever in the state they couldn't walk to. They made friends wherever they went, and picnics became their staple activity.

Angelo admired and commended his wife for her desire to honor her parents' sacrifice, and to give an alternate life-path to her brothers and sisters. Together they did what they could to secure visas for the first two of Maggie's siblings to join them in New York.

"Let them all come, they are welcome in our home!" Angelo had declared, causing Maggie's love for her husband to compound daily.

Emilia slept in Eleanor's old room, and Santiago slept on the couch. The little apartment was bursting at the seams, but so were their hearts, with joy and high spirits.

In the fall of 1962, Olivia joined them—a twin bed was added to Emilia's room and soon they taught her the ropes too, following the same steps they all had in applying for resident status, obtaining a work permit, securing a job, and registering for English classes.

Maggie kept house for all of them. She attended school in the evening, but for interior decorating this time. Talk of larger living quarters began, and a plan was laid out to save for it—surely, next *sprimmer* would find them in a three-bedroom apartment!

Weeks went happily by, in a flurry of hard work, laughter, and sharing of their dreams. In her daily prayers, Maggie credited the angels for her wedded bliss, and for how Angelo and her siblings genuinely appreciated each other.

"Ordained by the heavens," Maggie would often say to herself. Nothing could tarnish their enchanted lives.

As Halloween approached—Olivia's first experience with the holiday—Maggie dipped into the household's savings jar and bought colorful capes and witch's hats for her sisters, she already had hers. Angelo and Santiago would wear white sheets tied at the wrists, ankles, and waist. She had markers with which to color black spots on the sheets to resemble a Dalmatian's coat—they had all seen and loved the movie released earlier in the year.

Carrying a bulky bag with the costumes and humming to Helen Shapiro's, *You Don't Know*, Maggie stopped to collect their mail. As soon as she opened the mailbox, she noted a stack of letters, the size of a brick. Frowning, Maggie pulled out the package tied with a black ribbon, the return address leapt from a corner of the topmost envelope, as did the postmark, stabbing her heart.

A. Navarro, July 1962.

Maggie couldn't breathe, she stared at the packet in her hand, its weight seemed to become that of an actual brick. *Alonzo did write to me!*

Weakened by the unexpected blow, Maggie leaned against the wall and slid to a crouching position.

The tip of a witch hat peeked at her from the bag next to her, mocking her.

"Someone kept these from me!" Maggie realized with another shock, "But, who?"

Lourdes readily came to mind, causing a surge of hatred toward the horrid woman and her son. But either because Maggie's legs had fallen asleep while crouching against the wall, or because her body could not abide such dark reaction toward Lourdes, a wave of nausea swept through Maggie. It stopped at the top of her throat paralyzing her, she could not get sick in public!

She closed her eyes and took a deep breath—she must calm her thoughts. Maybe it wasn't even Lourdes who had done it. But if not her—impossible to think Eleanor could do such a thing—could Angelo have asked her to?

Every cell in her body cried out in protest. Maggie might retch in the empty hallway after all. She opened her eyes and pushed herself up the wall to a standing position. "No."

Maggie dragged herself out to the alley where a couple of boys were smoking cigarettes.

Catching one of their furtive glances, Maggie said in a voice that, to her, sounded disembodied, "May I borrow your matches?"

Something came over her. She watched herself, as if from afar, setting down the bag with the Halloween costumes, placing the stack of letters on the lip of the dumpster, striking the match, and its resulting combustion. She grabbed the stack of letters, estimating that there must be about forty, *he wrote every week*! With a shaking hand, she placed the lit match under them.

Maggie held on, even as the outer ones separated from the whole, like flickering dark feathers. She turned them this way and that, letting the flames consume the unread words. The tears came, and she let them. *Only until his words are reduced to ashes*, she told herself.

Nothing in Alonzo's letters could change the fact that she was married to a man she loved. As to who had stolen her letters, and why they had chosen to return them now, Maggie rejected the effort of investigating that twisted mystery as a waste of her energies.

Unable to resist the heat of the steady flame any longer, she dropped the blazing clump. Maggie's mind triumphed over her heart again; she had not indulged her curiosity.

The tips of her fingers bore the sooty marks of Alonzo's promise, and on an impulse, she brought them to her lips.

She blew a kiss to the smoldering ashes at the bottom of the dumpster.

"Hey," she called, and tossed the matchbook to the boy, "thanks."

Maggie picked up the Halloween bag on her way back inside, where life would go on, as would her family.

Chapter 17

With heavy step, Maggie crossed the hallway toward their apartment. She would not tell Angelo, or her siblings, about the letters having ever existed—anyway, they were really gone now, and she hadn't read them.

I didn't read them! screamed her mind, perplexed by the decision. Had she not fretted for weeks about Alonzo breaking his promise to write to her? The tears came again, angry and frustrated, for Alonzo had not broken faith with her. It tortured her to wonder what her actions might have been if the letters had been returned before she married. She had pledged herself to Alonzo first!

Throwing the door closed behind her, Maggie promised this would be the only secret she would ever keep from her husband, *it's not as disloyal as if I had read the letters!*

Devilish thoughts followed her into the sunny front room, for Maggie was still nowhere near banishing the incident from her mind, but she was determined not to let it touch her heart.

Glad that no one would be home for a couple of hours, Maggie dropped the bag with the costumes by the coat rack and removed her coverings, taunting herself, *was I coward not to read them?*

Was I afraid that on confirming Alonzo's devotion, and that he kept his promise, I would regret marrying Angelo? Maggie sat at the dining table; eyes fixed on a place far beyond the walls of her home. *No!*

She moved on to question whether meeting Angelo had indeed been divine providence, or had there been sinister forces at work instead?

From where she sat, silent and still, Maggie saw a glimmer of truth winking at her. It seemed to be just out of her range of understanding, buried under thousands of Hail Marys and religious rituals, she gleaned from it only that her choices had been right and there was no turning back the clock.

The greater truth, that Angelo's coming into her life had been ordained by the stars, for the fruits of Maggie's womb would brook no other origins, eluded her.

What if Angelo had the letters all along? she persisted, although in a dark corner of her mind, Maggie knew this was likely how the devil might sow doubt between a man and his wife. *What if he gave them back to test me, to know what I would do with them?*

If she said nothing, would Angelo tear their home apart looking for a likely hiding place? Drive himself crazy imagining her stealing away in the night to read another man's love letters. *Unthinkable!*

"I will see evidence of it in his eyes tonight."

Angelo's brown eyes would not lie—if he had done it as some sort of wicked test, Maggie would know.

Her shoulders relaxed. She let her doubts trail behind her as she went into the bathroom to wash her face. From the mirror, a wan face looked back at her, two smoky fingerprints still marked her lips. A sob escaped but she stifled the others by splashing icy water on her face. She must banish every thought about Alonzo.

"I won't regret, I won't wallow. What's done is done!"

Maggie patted her face dry with a towel. To her reflection, she said, "I love my husband. I love my family. That is my only truth."

That evening, amidst the rowdy preparations for the Halloween party, from beneath the brim of her witch's hat, Maggie sought Angelo's eyes as he came out of their bedroom.

Be it that a Dalmatian, on its hind legs, couldn't possibly conceive of evil schemes, or that her husband's eyes spoke plainly about such plots never crossing his mind, a satisfied smile flowered on her lips, soothing her troubles with its warm radiance.

In the center of the vault that was Maggie's heart, sat the intact pack of letters tied with a ribbon. She slammed the vault shut, never to be opened again.

Chapter
18

M aggie delighted in how the passage of time revealed the rhyme and reason for everything. When angels had guided her to delay accepting Alonzo's proposal, she knew in her heart that family came first, and it became her truth from then on.

What she had perceived as doom, was nothing but the end of one thing and the beginning of something else. She could not overlook the recurring proof of doors closing only to have windows thrown wide open in other chambers of her life. And who was doing the opening and closing? Why, the angels, of course, because the stars were inanimate objects after all.

While the Gemini constellation danced in the heavens in 1963, Maggie conceived her first child.

During the three weeks it took for her to realize she was pregnant, the Twins had ample time to marvel at the new life springing into the world, for this was a family line they had influenced before, and would do so again, while they had dominion of the sky.

Of the many cosmic gifts in The Twins' repertoire, they chose to imprint upon Maggie's first child the ability to transmute practical

energy into empathy. And with that, quite pleased with themselves, they left the embryo to replicate the imprint on its proliferating cells.

Maggie was home alone when she learned that a new life stirred in her womb. She treasured the knowledge for every second of the three hours it would take for her family to return from work. She sat on the couch, palms on her belly, fancying she could detect the microscopic being inside.

Unaware of The Twins' work, Maggie started her own beginner brand of imprinting, exactly as she had seen Dolores do. Maggie spoke to the child within, reassuring it that a loving family of her own awaited. Without knowing it, she threaded the assurance with a gift all her own and which had served her well: far-seeing intuition.

As the afternoon darkened, and to contain her excitement, Maggie distracted herself by preparing a feast. She knew well that for happiness to multiply, it must be shared, so only when everyone was home and sitting at the table, did she reveal the news of the baby.

The already happy household became jubilant. The father-to-be, aunts-to-be, uncle-to-be were beside themselves with elation, and a radiant Maggie mirrored all their expressions.

The residents of the small dwelling resumed their routines with an undeniable sense of heightened bliss. For Maggie, that first conversation with her belly, at the edge of her bed in the quiet apartment, became a daily ritual that gave her purpose. She kept it up until the fourth day in March 1964, when their daughter arrived, just as winter began to give way to spring.

Angelo could not have been happier with his wife and daughter. He named the baby, Raquel, but by the end of their first day back at home, passed from doting aunts to doting uncle, her name had been shortened to Kelly—a nickname that followed her into adulthood.

To Angelo, Maggie said nothing, but to her sisters, who after their first exposure to Halloween had begun calling themselves the merry witches, she bemoaned the modern circumstances that kept her from doing as Dolores had taught them.

"It's just as well I didn't get a little piece of the placenta. Even if they had considered it at the hospital, we have no garden to bury it in."

Being the couple's first, Kelly assimilated the undiluted love of the family, with all its pros and cons. On account of the gifts of empathy and intuition driving her, even at nine-months old, Kelly's lively yellow eyes could read her family's body language and accents, seeming to sympathize with the wide range of moods in the household.

But it was more than that, the little girl's ability had a supernatural reach too. Indeed, on a stormy night at the end of April, it was only Kelly who heard Taurus' deep bellow—it woke her from a sound sleep. Holding on to the crib's rail, she stood on wobbly legs and listened intently until, like thunder, the sound rolled away.

Kelly laid back down, drowsily sucking on her pacifier, and dreamt of shooting stars nesting in her momma's belly.

Taurus continued to stomp and grumble in the sky, with the stubborn purpose to spread harmony and stability over the weeks that are The Bull's to survey. Maggie and Angelo's second child would enter the world with a latent desire to achieve those qualities.

Out of nowhere, never experienced migraines came to plague Maggie, disrupting the intuitive awareness of her body. She was seven weeks along when she discovered their second child was on the way.

Believing the new pregnancy was the reason behind the fiendish headaches, Maggie side-stepped her morning discomforts in favor of a more productive, evening imprinting ritual for her baby.

Once again, the entire household became invested in preparations for the new arrival, making the isolating torment of the migraines more bearable for Maggie who, influenced by the upcoming move, had engaged in an altruistic transference with her belly. Whenever the pain lifted, Maggie sang to it about freedom from expectations, and about discovering true paths.

In the fall of 1965, child number two road-tripped from the east to the west coast in Maggie's womb. Some of their friends, who had already settled there, not only suggested the move but, helped them get oriented in the western state.

The holidays found them employed and set up in a three-bedroom single family home in Los Angeles county, complete with front and backyard.

Maggie looked forward to having a garden again!

The never-failing presence of the sun was an indescribable improvement to Maggie's mind—she realized what a mild paradise California was compared to the extreme New York weather they'd left behind. Her mind soared with sun-drenched possibilities.

In the days leading up to the birth, Maggie and her sisters engaged in crafty discussions as to how the California doctor might come around to letting her have even a small piece of the placenta.

Angelo, on overhearing their plot, shot it down at once, "These are not witch-doctors in some Amazonian jungle!" he said, appalled.

As soon as he stormed out of the room, Maggie rounded on her sisters, "How is it that one of you isn't a doctor, or at least a nurse!"

The ladies laughed and agreed in whispers that it would be best to discuss the issue when Angelo wasn't around. It still came to naught, but Maggie would not lose hope of getting what she wanted.

Her feverish requests to the archangels intensified, and on January the thirty-first, at the appointed time, Angelo drove her to the hospital. She kissed him goodbye at the registration counter, from where a kindly nurse collected Maggie and wheeled her away to the maternity ward.

As luck, or the angels, would have it, the nurse's Hispanic accent put Maggie at ease. Fancying she could see the light of divine intervention; she addressed her in their common native language.

After sharing where she was from, and how this was her second child, Maggie went on to say, "Back in Santa Victoria, the farm where I was born, my mother kept a garden. In it, she buried the placenta of every one of her children." Maggie knew she had struck a chord when she felt the nurse's warm hand squeezing her shoulder.

She pressed on, "Mine grew into a beautiful rose bush—"

How long had it been since she had thought about her white roses? Maggie would turn twenty-seven soon, would there be that many roses on the bush? Who would pick them? Who would notice?

"Señora Maggie," whispered the nurse, "if you can believe it, in my town women will eat a bite or two of the placenta."

Maggie wasn't surprised. "I've heard that before, we all adopt the practices we learn from our parents, don't we?"

They came out of the elevator into a long empty hallway, at the end of which was a swinging double door with frosted glass windows. The sign above it read, MATERNITY.

Halfway to their destination, the nurse leaned in and whispered again, "Señora Maggie, don't worry. I will get you a little piece of it for your garden."

Warm gratitude spread through Maggie's limbs. She reached over her shoulder and the nurse squeezed Maggie's proffered hand, sealing their agreement.

A few hours later, on that Monday morning, when Maggie awoke after the C-section, the first face she saw was that of the kindly nurse.

Pressing her hand on Maggie's forehead, as if checking her temperature, she murmured, "It's in your coat pocket."

Maggie closed her eyes, a faint 'God bless you' escaped her lips before she drifted off to sleep.

As soon as they were allowed, Angelo and the rest of the household gathered round mother and baby. Angelo took the infant from Maggie and rocked her, focused on the small face as if trying to hear something the baby was saying. His expression cleared after a few moments, and with a proud smile, he announced to the room at large, "This is, Elizabeth."

Exhausted, Maggie relaxed as she listened to the approving sounds circling her bed.

Cradling the baby in turn, Olivia beamed, "The thirty-first of January is the Day of Poetic Song."

"Do tell us, what else do the stars have to say about this," Santiago teased, causing everyone to snicker about Olivia's latest obsession with Astrology.

Undeterred, though with a pointed roll of her eyes, Olivia went on to say, "Monday was named after the moon, by the ancients, because the lunar energy drives people born on that day of the week. Lizzy—"

Emilia jumped in right away, "Already nick-naming the baby?"

"She's Lizzy," Olivia shrugged, "and not only was she born under the influence of the moon, but Aquarius is the bearer of truth and wisdom. There's no telling what Lizzy will do in her life."

As she listened to her sister, something stirred in Maggie's recently vacated womb—the angels and Mary seemed to be skeptically shaking their heads, while the nuns outright condemned Olivia's statements. Maggie put her hand over her belly to ease the disquiet and decided, on the spot, that Lizzy would be baptized as soon as she could get herself to church. And Emilia would be Lizzy's merry-god-witch—*I mean, godmother!*

She entrusted Emilia with the seed-sized placenta in its plastic baggie. By the time Maggie returned home with Lizzy, a couple of days later, there was a terra cotta pot with fresh soil, on the kitchen's windowsill.

Following her sister's glance, Olivia said, "We won't know what will sprout from it for at least eight weeks."

The months following Lizzy's arrival were a whirlwind of productivity, family bonding, and development. The lively Southern California household included Maggie, Angelo, their two daughters, and six of Maggie's brothers and sisters. A crowded, happy home that shared expenses, chores, joys, and disappointments.

Amid the sweet chaos, the placenta in the pot germinated, and when Lizzy was six months old the merry-god-witches at last identified the bright green leaves as belonging to a Lilac bush.

At around that same time, the Lion paused in the heavens to watch The Virgin enter the celestial plane of influence. The cusping constellations held a few days' civil conference over Maggie's third child—there would be no more after this one.

The cells replicated for forty-eight hours while Leo transitioned out, leaving a star-studded gift of 'service' and 'leadership', which Virgo complemented with 'gracious diplomacy' as she settled for her thirty-day stint in the astral sphere.

Suspecting this might be her last child, after all, she was nearing thirty years of age, Maggie sang daily to her belly about love, trust in divine providence, and loyalty, that they would become the driving purpose of the new baby's life.

Maggie's third daughter arrived before noon on a Tuesday. It was May the thirtieth, in the year of our Lord, 1967.

This baby's reception was no different than the other two. Promptly after work, father, uncles and merry-god-witches appeared bedside. Angelo was first to hold his child, and after a moments' conference with the baby, he presented, Marie.

All those present commended his choice as Angelo handed the baby to Olivia. She at once declared, "Tuesday is the perfect day for Marie to have been born!"

"Here we go," Emilia quipped, fussing with the baby's blanket while Olivia bounced her.

"But it's true! Tuesday is ruled by Mars—"

"That's the god of war, do we have a warrior in our hands?" Santiago teased.

"In mythology, yes. But for days of the week, Mars means action. Marie will persist and achieve whatever goals and dreams she sets her heart to."

Her mind to—whatever goals she sets her mind to, Maggie corrected inwardly.

"May thirtieth puts Marie under the influence of Gemini, and although she doesn't look it—I mean, she's only hours old—she'll be quick witted and silver-tongued," Olivia persisted, lowering Marie to where Kelly could see her.

Kelly smiled, dimples flashing on her cheeks, as she gently patted the baby's head.

"What do you say, Lizzy?"

From her perch in Santiago's arms, Lizzy looked on her new sister with furrowed brow, appearing more warrior-like than sweet, brown-eyed Marie ever could, and said nothing.

With a complacent smile on her face, Maggie watched the proceedings. Even though there had been no accommodating nurse during Marie's birth, to sneak a cut of the placenta, nothing marred Maggie's gut sense of having completed an important mission—all felt right with the universe.

She had three God-given children, whom she loved with all her heart.

Because she had carried them for nine months, she naively felt she already knew them. Surely, mild guidance from her was all they needed to become the women Maggie had envisioned.

Chapter 19

Ten years after her exciting arrival in New York, a more mature Maggie reflected on how, over the course of a decade, she had more than honored her parents' sacrifice. True, she had pleased herself along the way by marrying a man she loved, but Angelo loved her so fully that he embraced her siblings as his own. And in doing so, he helped bring Maggie's dearest wish to fruition; opening the same doors for her siblings that Vicente and Dolores had opened for her.

An indistinct whisper, aimed at the depths of a locked vault in her heart, hinted that Alonzo could not have been that mate. And warmed anew by the satisfaction of her inspired choices along the way, Maggie marveled at how light and lovely life stretched before her.

Only two of the original merry-god-witches remained, the other siblings had either married or returned to their home country. Kelly was already of pre-school age, and Lizzy and Marie would be old enough too, at the snap of a finger. She and Angelo would begin a new stage, just the two of them, as their little family took on the coming years.

Maggie finally had her interior decorating certificate and was looking forward to making an independent career of it. But her rosy visions were dashed following an extended visit from two of Angelo's uncles.

Due to one of them being quite ill, they had decided to bring him to California for treatment, though much too late. In the end, only one gentleman returned as the bearer of tragic news for the family back home.

There must have been phone calls. Pressure must have been applied by the rest of Angelo's family, but for weeks after the old gentleman's departure, Maggie never heard about any of it. Until one fine morning, when Angelo announced, with shocking finality, that the time had come to return to their home country.

The earth seemed to shake.

"I didn't think going back to South America was even a consideration for us," Maggie pleaded, aghast, "we have a new house here. The girls' future is here, ours too. Isn't that what we were working toward? You're throwing all that away?"

"Why on earth would we not have a future or a roof over our heads back in our hometown?" Angelo replied, irritably.

"It couldn't possibly match what we have achieved here! We have potential in this country, over there—what are the opportunities for someone like me?" Maggie's voice trembled as she said the words, so vivid was the flash of the struggles that awaited them. She knew no women there with independent careers—only wives and mothers.

"You're just thinking of yourself. What about me, what about what I want?"

Maggie's thoughts swirled so fast in her head that she felt dizzy. *No! This can't be happening!*

"But that's just it—you never even hinted there was a possibility we would go back!" A wave of nausea washed over her as she wondered if indeed, she was being selfish. But no, it was quite the opposite. When pressed, Angelo had categorically stated there was enough bad blood with the elders in his family as to make it impossible for him to return.

"Why so sudden a change? Why don't we think about it, as a couple, responsible for providing the best future for our daughters?"

Apparently, reminding her husband that there were three more people to consider in the decision, was the wrong thing to say.

"I am going back. You and the girls can come, if you like. It makes no difference to me."

"What has gotten into you?" Maggie demanded, thunderstruck, "how have I misunderstood our path? Do you not care how depressing it will be to leave my sisters and brother, set up for the bright existence we were supposed to have been at the center of?"

"I have assurances of work and a place to live. Our potential will not be materially damaged, rather it will improve. And besides, it is time I patch up differences with my family."

Maggie mistrusted the supposed assurances but if they existed, as tangible facts, she could not ignore them.

The scale tipped: after all Angelo had done to help her own family, she couldn't possibly begrudge him efforts on behalf of his! Also, divorce, was not a word in Maggie's vocabulary, nor would she have her girls grow up without a father.

Yet even if it hadn't been on purpose, Maggie felt she'd been manipulated into the life-changing decision sweeping her away from a cherished vision. Dark words, such as perfidy and treachery, reared their dissenting heads when she thought about all that her husband was forcing her to give up.

Maggie indulged in the sudden bitterness with relish, but only until she glimpsed the gulf of regret it might lead to. She chose to take the power from Angelo and manage the situation as if it had been her decision all along.

Although disenchanted anew that her dream of uniting her entire family in California had come to nothing, Maggie began to coordinate their return.

"You must rally your spirits," Emilia soothed, while Maggie sniffled, "focus on the positive; mom and dad are there, as are the rest of our siblings."

Maggie dabbed her eyes with a tissue. "Yes. And there's the rest of his family to get acquainted with. So far, I've met his uncle, and a sister with her two kids. Remember when they came to New York? What a chaotic visit that was!"

"Kelly was barely a year old," Emilia said with a reminiscent nod.

"Who's to say, that life in our hometown won't be as nice as here!" Maggie muttered, rising from the chair and giving Emilia a tight hug.

With a dull step and a heavy heart, Maggie began the process of sorting and marking their belongings to be packed, shipped, or donated. She wondered what circles they'd move in. A bitter feeling returned when she remembered with distaste, the rigid social levels

people lived by in the capital—so stuffy and conventional compared to the last ten years of the most delightful sense of equality, freedom, and such wondrous prospects.

Soon there was nothing left to do; their clothing and a handful of household items had been packed, furniture and appliances had been crated, and whatever remained had been divvyed up between Maggie's siblings, everything except for Lizzy's Lilac bush.

"Please, transplant it to a larger pot as it grows," Maggie entrusted Olivia with the task.

"I'll look after it and won't ever part with it."

Maggie wore white that day in 1969 when she boarded the plane. The girls had been dressed like dolls by their merry-god-witches, Kelly in purple, her long hair arranged in lovely finger curls. Lizzy in blue, her hair was so thick and curly the aunts couldn't do anything but stick a bow on it. And Marie, a true dolly in brown overalls stamped with daisies.

Bitter tears were shed, even by Kelly, who at five years old was already a consummate empath. Lizzy and Marie didn't understand what was happening but could feel it wasn't a day like the others, so they allowed themselves to be hugged and kissed, while looking on everyone with bemused concern.

What a difference ten years had made, indeed.

The last time Maggie had gotten on a plane it was with the lightness of spirit of a young lady, excited about a new adventure, clutching a new purse—a symbol of her parents' sacrifice and trust in her. Here was a thwarted Maggie, climbing on an airplane for the second time in her life, to return to the place she'd come from.

She hitched Marie snugly on her hip, and held Kelly's hand as she followed Angelo, who had Lizzy in his arms, onto the tarmac to board the plane.

As they made their way down the aisle to their seats, blinking away the tears, a celestial wave of gratitude overwhelmed her—impossible to describe the weight of disappointment battling the buoyancy of spirit that invaded her. Then and there, Maggie buried all selfish, negative feelings, they were of no use to her.

Thank you for my children, for my husband, and thank you, that I will soon be able to embrace my parents.

Chapter

20

As planned, they were received by Angelo's sister, Nora, her husband, Raul, and their children—the same ones Maggie had met in New York. They must impose on them until Angelo's work and their new residence were sorted out.

Alas, those two critical objectives failed to manifest as planned. Shortly after making the required calls, a humiliated Angelo had to confess to his wife that it had all been a ploy by the elders.

"There is no job, and no place for us to live," he said, unable to look Maggie in the eyes.

The news knocked the wind out of her. "But you assured me! You said our prospects would not change—that's what you said—and now we're homeless?"

The broken faith and the impotence of her circumstances fueled a quiet rage within Maggie. If she could not look at Angelo, with the kind of trust her little girls saw in her, how on earth could she believe in him again?

Had Maggie suspected as much, she would have given more thought to a separation or a divorce. As it were, the betrayed captive could do nothing but try to rationalize her circumstances. *Speculations, like regrets*, she lectured herself, *are the evil darkness that only wastes my energy. I refuse to dwell in that darkness—I won't lend my ear to the devil.*

While Angelo and Raul reviewed opportunities for work, Maggie decided to take some action herself. She called in a favor at her old school and, in the process, discovered that the old building she and her sisters had attended, had become a residence for the nuns, while the school had moved to a new building.

The current Mother Superior granted Maggie a special circumstances tuition, and Kelly was enrolled in Kindergarten that very day. The little girl was expected to attend in less than a month, when the new school year kicked off.

That accomplishment gave Maggie a short-lived respite from her upended existence.

Within a couple of days, Angelo was offered a job, thanks to Raul's contacts, and husband and wife experienced a sense of things beginning to stabilize.

Still, how Maggie longed to have a home of her own instead of just one room in someone else's house.

Overnight, it seemed, that longing was also addressed.

"My uncle has come around and has agreed to let us live in one of his properties."

"Oh. That is good news," Maggie whispered, distrustful. She had put the girls down for the evening, but she could hear them tossing and turning on the other side of the partition. "I hope it won't be too far from your work, or from Kelly's school."

The grim look in his brown eyes spoke volumes. Maggie frowned, "Where is this property?"

"It's outside the city—about an hour or two north of here. It's a country estate."

"Should I not have registered Kelly for school—is there a school she can attend over there? What will we do about a car for you to get to and from work?" Maggie's concerns tumbled one over the other, anxious to visualize what the future held.

Angelo shook his head. "There are only indigenous people around the property, and I don't think there are any schools. I do remember there being a small-town square and a church though."

"What will we do then?"

"We'll figure something out," Angelo offered, "should be no trouble finding a used car and we'll go from there."

It was hardly the level of assurance she would have liked, but the isolated location described by her husband had begun to intrigue Maggie. A country estate did sound grand, could that make the remoteness of it more palatable? Her curiosity was roused.

Their belongings were not due to arrive for another three weeks, but Maggie felt relieved to have an end in sight to their imposition on Angelo's sister and her family.

With renewed vigor, she exerted every effort to make herself, and her children, as pleasant and helpful as possible for the next several days.

"Do you think we could go see the country estate this weekend?" Maggie proposed, her stance softening the longer she had to process it, "our things will be arriving within seven days and it might be a good idea to clean and fix anything that needs fixing."

Angelo nodded, "I was thinking the same thing. I will talk to my uncle and we can make an outing of it!"

Maggie played down her anticipation as the party of seven piled into Raul's dual cab truck. Angelo rode up front with Nora and Raul, and Maggie took the bench seat in back. She carried Marie on her lap, Kelly and Lizzy sat on either side of her. They were to meet Angelo's uncle at the property.

A sense of foreboding began to cloud Maggie's sunny mood as signs of civilization gave way to open fields and rolling hills covered with Eucalyptus trees. Picturesque though it was, the scenery and the passage of time impressed upon Maggie just how remote their new home would be.

The impossibility of Angelo driving Kelly to Kindergarten, every day, also dawned on her—where would she stay until he finished work and could bring her home? She held tight to Marie while gathering Kelly close to her. Lizzy stood on tiptoes, holding on to the backrest of the front seat so she could look at the road ahead.

The paved highway ended shortly after they passed the city limits.

They had been on the gravel road longer than an hour when, at last, Raul slowed down to make a left turn.

Sitting up straighter, to see where they were headed, Maggie spied a narrow dirt road, with a ravine on one side and a cliff on the other. The roots protruding from it and the deep erosion marks told Maggie that that section would be a mudslide problem in the rainy season.

"Looks like our uncle is already up there," Angelo said, pointing to the fresh tire marks on the cocoa powder-like dirt. As they started up the treacherous road he added, "Time to roll up the windows."

The interior of the cab became stuffy at once. Despite the windows being closed, the fine dust found its way in. The girls began to fuss, looking to Maggie for an idea as to when the discomfort would end.

"Look at the beautiful tunnel the trees make!" Maggie pointed out for the benefit of her girls. Kelly and Marie looked out obligingly, but Lizzy wasn't interested—her cheeks were red, which meant she was hot and cranky. "We're almost there," Maggie said, assuming it couldn't be much longer if Nora was already touching up her lipstick—a difficult task when being knocked about inside the truck, on a road full of potholes.

They made another left turn onto a small lane. They drove alongside an adobe fence on the right and alfalfa fields on the left, until they arrived at an open iron gate. They turned right and proceeded up a driveway, paved with stone and lined by ancient looking pine trees.

Lizzy's perennial frown cleared as she pointed a chubby finger up ahead, looking at Maggie for a reaction.

"Yes, isn't that lovely!" Maggie said of the whitewashed fountain topped with a cherub. Behind it stood an impressive stone house with stucco arches and window frames. They passed the cherub fountain and parked at the bottom of the split staircase, which led up to the main entrance of the house.

Angelo helped the girls and Maggie out of the back seat. She stretched her back, allowing a moment to take in the majestic sight, and compose herself.

Formal greetings were exchanged all around. Maggie noticed that Angelo's uncle had brought along one of the maids, she was busy opening the wood shutters inside, presumably to air out the house.

They were led, as a group, away from the house and around the circular driveway, remarking on the trees and shrubs nearby, pointing out the things that needed fixing on the detached garage and caretaker room behind it. When they got to the back, they discussed the care of the gated garden, all the while, Angelo's uncle lamented the difficulties of finding and keeping reliable help.

"But how wonderful that family will be at hand now, to oversee the upkeep of the estate," the old gentleman declared.

Maggie saw the garden's potential at once. In a glittering haze of sunshine and chirping birds she saw the girls playing there, while she tended to the beautiful flowers!

As if guessing her thoughts, Angelo squeezed her hand and she returned the pressure.

Certainly, they would go into the house next, but Angelo's uncle led them on a narrow path instead. It took them across an alfalfa field to a ramshackle adobe house, whose stone foundation doubled as a storage shed. They walked around this rectangular structure too. Angelo's uncle explained that behind the three sets of wooden doors, they'd find all manner of gardening and construction tools, along with old furniture that had been moved out of the big house.

Something in the old man's tone and demeanor, caused a cold inkling to seep into Maggie's mind. She glanced at her husband, with the question in her eyes, but he took no note, respectfully absorbed as he was in the one-way conversation.

"The stairs over here will need to get repaired, but one of the locals should be able to help you with that. In the meantime, you can use a ladder to get in through the kitchen."

Maggie watched Angelo's face as it transfigured, from attentive concentration to terminal disappointment. She almost felt sorry for him—almost—her own bitter experience with their trickery and manipulation was too recent to allow it.

Working through her own agitation, Maggie continued to listen and glance where directed, realizing with disgust that Angelo would not fight it, any of it. Every feeling inside revolted at the injury, she wished it was her place to rebuke it, after all, with Angelo having to work in the city, it would be her, Maggie, the one being relegated to caretaker!

That her husband put his head down and submitted to such treatment was a new blow to her—in this new version of Angelo, she lost sight of the dashing man she had met and married in New York.

Maggie scooped Marie up and held her hand out to Kelly, "Let's look at the pretty flowers over here," she trilled, drawing away from the group and humming an indistinct tune to placate her mutinous feelings.

Lizzy twisted in her father's arms to see where her sisters were going, and Angelo set her down, seemingly glad to be relieved of the burden.

The better to play the part of the dutiful, grateful-for-scraps nephew, Maggie thought viciously—her humming intensified.

She guided the girls to the nearest row of alfalfa plants and pointed out the velvety green leaves and lovely purple flowers, "Cows love alfalfa, it's their favorite."

On hearing that, Lizzy plucked a flower and put it in her mouth. Kelly and Marie watched their sister for a reaction, which came after Lizzy chewed on it twice.

"Ugh!" Lizzy began spitting it out, fishing bits of it out of her mouth with her fingers.

Maggie smiled patiently as she pulled a tissue out of her purse to wipe her daughter's chin.

"Water," Lizzy gagged.

"We are going back to the car," Maggie called out in the general direction of the group. She took off without pausing for their acknowledgment, they were still standing around their uncle, in rapt, deferential silence.

As they made their way down the lane, Maggie began humming a children's song, which Kelly recognized. The innocent voice joined Maggie's defiant one as they trudged back to the car, away from the spectacle of her husband's defeat.

How am I to recover from this—do I even want to?

Chapter
21

During the long drive back to the city, Maggie spoke to the girls, to Nora and to Raul, but not to her husband. The condition of the roads, the distance, the beauty of the grounds, the elegant estate, the potential of the caretaker's house—their future home—were thoroughly remarked on by all, except Angelo.

Maggie took his brooding silence to mean he was ashamed, as well he should, for failing to stand up for his wife and children! Perhaps now he regretted his decision to uproot them from their sunny home.

She knew Angelo well enough to know she must not say 'I told you so,' but what if she could induce a karmic redemption?

A glint of hope brightened her mood. Why, they could sell all their things as soon as they arrived from port, and they could buy tickets to get right back to California!

Maggie spent the rest of the drive to Nora and Raul's imagining her spectacular return to the land where they could resume the pursuit of their happiness.

The girls were exhausted from the day-long outing and shortly after dinner, Maggie put them down for the night. They fell asleep on the other side of the partition, and only Kelly stirred when Maggie and Angelo began a conversation in tense whispers.

"It will be difficult, but nothing has been done that can't be undone," Maggie said as if she and her husband were on the same page.

"What do you think needs undoing?"

The tone of derision made it clear to Maggie that his thoughts had not journeyed along the same path as hers. "This whole trip—our prospects here are not ideal for our family, that was made evident today, don't you think?"

"How so? We will have a roof over our heads, I will have sufficient income."

"You can't mean that! You will bury the girls, and me, in that broken down shed in the middle of nowhere? How will Kelly get her schooling? And Lizzy will be ready to start soon too."

"I've already talked with my sister, and they will be able to keep Kelly here—they'll get her to school and back."

The words struck Maggie like a slap.

"So, there will be no consulting my feelings or opinion on becoming separated from my children? You will dispose of my time and energy as you would with a common laborer, with no say in the matter?"

"You chose to come," he lashed out.

The shock disfigured Maggie's face. She leaned away from him, stung.

Out of the corner of her eye, she saw his shoulders drop, it even seemed he might reach out and touch her, but he did not.

"It is not what I expected—it is certainly not what was promised—but I will get a used car soon, and if we make do for now, we will be able to afford a second vehicle for you before we know it. Truth be told, I'm looking forward to living in the country as opposed to the city."

Maggie averted her eyes and blinked away the tears, still not ready to see things from his point of view, or anyone's but her own. In mute rebellion, refusing to appeal to the virgin Mary or the angels, Maggie revisited the worst moments of the past three weeks, purposely fueling her displeasure and amplifying the breach between her and Angelo.

How she wished she could discuss the situation with her parents or her sisters. *But homeless people can't incur in the expense of long-distance calling*, she brooded, ignoring his attempts to talk up the purchase of a used car, and the prospect of living in a hovel.

Knowing that their argument wasn't over, Maggie rejoined with measured contempt, "I chose to come because you are my husband and my place is with you. And our children are treasures lent to us," she said, trusting the words came straight from the heavens, to ease the anxiety she felt over the upcoming separation. "We are to love, care and provide for them until they can fly on their own."

Angelo said nothing, but his glance met hers when a tiny sob came from the other side of the partition.

Maggie's eyes narrowed. She listened for a moment, then tiptoed over there to check. Lizzy and Marie slept soundly, but Kelly rolled onto her belly, groggily enough so that it seemed to Maggie she was asleep too.

I'm doing to Kelly what Angelo did to me. Maggie realized, and frowned at the fleeting notion that her decisions meant such a huge change for her eldest. *Kelly, the tiny radar who picks up signals from every soul in her vicinity! How will she fare in a home that isn't her own?*

Watching the sleeping girls, Maggie's eyes misted over, not ready to consider that she could expand her limits and operate outside the norms she had been taught. Instead, she resigned herself, and Kelly, to the inevitable hardships all humans must endure.

I survived separation too, she thought, accepting the stab of guilt she felt she deserved.

Chapter
22

After a hurried cup of coffee and toasted bread in the kitchen, Maggie waved goodbye to her husband. It was his first day at the new job and as soon as he left, she experienced the shift in the household's energy. Angelo was the buffer, giving Maggie and the girls license to be there. With him gone, even if just for the day, she felt like an unwanted burden at her sister-in-law's house.

A flicker of pity for little Kelly hit her anew, she saw her daughter's lively yellow eyes lost in a somber stone building full of nuns, and her only respite after a long day, would be returning to an adult household.

Kelly's dimpled smile pierced Maggie's heart, causing a ripple of change to start.

The longed-for call from the trucking company, announcing the arrival of their things, came the next day, throwing the family into a whirlwind of activity. The container had arrived at port, but it needed to clear customs before the cargo could get loaded into a truck. In all, they had about five days to make the caretaker's house inhabitable.

128

"I can't very well take off work when I've just started," Angelo argued that night over dinner, "by now though, the walls should be patched as my uncle said they would be."

"Yes!" Nora confirmed, "he called yesterday to say all the place needed was maybe some paint."

Maggie helped Marie with her potatoes, not saying a word. Why hadn't Nora shared the news with her?

I'm not her sibling, that's why!

If Maggie hadn't come with her husband, he would, of course, live with his sister for as long as it took to afford a place of his own. For all she knew, the far-flung housing was the family's way of punishing her, for following her husband and becoming an imposition on the lot of them.

Had Angelo's intention, all along, been to abandon her and the girls?

Impossible!

Sick of speculating and feeling helpless, Maggie decided to take her future head-on. At that moment, she wanted nothing more than to be left to her own devices.

To Raul, she said, "I know it is such a long drive, but would it be possible for you to take me, and the girls, with our things day after tomorrow?"

"So soon?"

"Well, yes! Tomorrow I'll shop for supplies and basic food items that won't spoil. And in two days, I can have the place clean and ready for when our things arrive," Maggie declared, sealing her resolve to regain some control of her situation.

"And I will have the truck follow me there on the weekend, to unload," Angelo said, with the first trace of genuine interest Maggie had heard in a long while.

If not for Kelly's looming fate, Maggie could almost look forward to the excitement of a new challenge.

The ripple of change continued to expand.

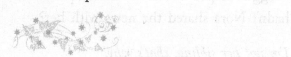

Maggie took a cab to the supermarket, without the girls, for it wasn't a leisurely outing. She combed the aisles putting items in the cart, checking them off the list she had prepared the night before, and tallying the subtotal.

As she entered the cleaning supply section, her mind took a sudden leap back to New York.

She stood staring at the brooms and mops hanging on display hooks. She reached for the wooden handle nearest to her, smiling as her fingers closed around it. Maggie became the green witch from a decade before! Her glance fell on the collection of matching mini brooms on the shelf, and her thoughts flitted to the little girls waiting for her.

Laughing under her breath, Maggie put three of them in the cart, not bothering to add them to the subtotal.

She threw in a bucket and mop before heading to the register, her mind completely rearranged by the cosmic connection of past and present, thanks to a silly broom!

With a ripple of pleasure, she reflected, that although Kelly, Lizzy and Marie might be borrowed, she, Maggie, had been entrusted with teaching them to fly. And she would do just that.

The dual cab truck had been loaded with Maggie's shopping from the day before, plus all the things they had brought with them on the plane, which included clothing, toiletries, and some books and toys for the girls.

After lunch, she and Raul topped it all off with a borrowed mattress, and a set of sheets. Blankets and pillows too, all of which would be returned as soon their own were set up.

They were ready to go.

Maggie radiated eager purpose. The girls were giddy with excitement—they had given up their brooms on the promise that they would get them back as soon as they arrived at their new place.

"I'm useless with housework," Nora excused herself from joining the party, and waved them off as they backed out of the driveway.

Maggie found herself falling into easy conversation with Raul—a genuinely helpful individual in whose company the two-hour drive seemed a lot shorter.

When they passed the lane leading to the iron gate and to the main house, the sense of injury resurfaced. But Maggie pushed it back deliberately as they continued up the road to their own entrance.

They pulled in amid a cloud of dust. When it settled, Maggie saw that the crooked wooden doors of the storage shed were thrown open.

"Looks like the worker we met the other day is here," Maggie said, eyeballing the adobe structure above that was to be their new home.

"Either him or a carpenter," Raul suggested, motioning toward a bucket with an assortment of tools sticking out of it, "it looks like they're repairing the stairs, so you might not have to use a ladder after all."

"That will be nice." Maggie looked around for the workers, but couldn't find them, "They're taking a break, I guess."

Raul turned the engine off, and they got out of the car. The girls took turns springing off the front seat, onto his arms, to be set down on the ground.

"Let's find the best way to get inside," Maggie proposed.

"My broom!" Marie said, pulling on Raul's sleeve, and he immediately obliged.

Maggie set off to inspect, followed by Raul and her ducklings, armed with their brooms. They found the two workers at the back of the house, enjoying the afternoon sun.

"Hello there," Maggie said, causing them to stand up respectfully, "I'm Mrs. Moretti."

"Good afternoon, yes, we were expecting someone would come soon. My name is Arlo, ma'am, and this is my cousin."

Maggie thought them agreeable enough. She listened as she followed them back to their work area and learned that the stone blocks, connecting the ground level to the upstairs floor, would be mortared by that night and dried by the next. In the meantime, there was a ladder on the other side and, yes, they would be happy to help unload.

"Mrs. Moretti, just so you know, the water isn't turned on, and even when it is, there isn't much pressure to make it upstairs. But we will make sure the barrel down here is full. I'll get a bucket, and water from the dike for you."

This was a setback. Maggie knew there'd be no power, but no running water was less manageable. She looked to Raul for ideas.

"The dike water is good for cleaning only. But I can drive into town—it's only a couple of miles away—and I'll bring potable water to last for a few days."

"Thank you so much!" Realizing she would have to boil that water to make it suitable for drinking, she added, "I'm so glad you loaned us your camping stove!" Not even during her childhood in Santa Victoria had she had to do that. Their water had come from a natural spring then.

"Be right back."

They watched him drive out slowly, stirring up as little dust as possible.

"Are we ready?" Maggie said to the girls, who all grinned in response.

Lizzy, who had been pretending her broom was a horse, mimicked Maggie and threw it over her shoulder. She led her daughters to the south side of the house, where a ladder stood against the wall.

"May as well make this place our own right away," Maggie said, taking the brooms from the girls. She climbed up the ladder and slid them onto the kitchen floor before returning to help Marie up. Kelly and Lizzy managed by themselves.

"It's not very pretty," Kelly said, holding her broom off the graying floorboards.

"Shh!" Lizzy frowned, urging Kelly to quiet down.

"What?"

"The people in here think their house is pretty," Lizzy whispered, squinting at the empty expanse.

"What people?" Maggie said, putting her hand on her middle child's shoulder.

"I don't know them, but they seem nice—they're just wondering what we're doing."

Marie clung to Maggie's leg. Kelly looked around trying to make out what her sister was talking about.

"How many people, Lizzy?"

"I only see two, momma, maybe there's more over there," Lizzy jutted her chin toward the wall dividing the kitchen from the rest of the place.

Maggie squared her shoulders and declared, "Well, then, with your leave!" she grabbed her broom, bowing respectfully to the room at large, and the girls followed suit, "we may not see eye to eye on 'pretty' but we can all agree that it needs to be cleaned!"

Their new rectangular living quarters consisted, lengthwise, of kitchen, master bedroom, bathroom, and a common room where the girls would sleep. Opposite that stretch of space was the dining room, family room and a receiving hall that connected with the steps under construction.

Having walked the length of the upstairs to the north end, Maggie announced, "This will be your room, and we will begin sweeping from here all the way back to the kitchen."

"We are not ever going to finish!" Lizzy cried disheartened, staring down the empty common room, "it goes on forever!"

"That's why there are four of us, so we can do it quicker," Maggie replied, tackling the floorboards as she spoke, "c'mon, do like I'm doing."

"I thought we were going to fly in these, like witches do on Halloween!" Kelly muttered, nevertheless following Maggie's instructions.

Lizzy frowned, "We'll fly when we're done cleaning, right?"

"It will feel like we're flying once we are good and tired from a hard day's work," Maggie said, correcting Marie's efforts.

Noting the suspicion on the faces of her older daughters, she looked at them with a raised brow. "Who told you that witches fly on brooms on Halloween night?"

Kelly's yellow eyes flashed, and her cheeks colored, "You did, yesterday."

"Oh! Maybe I did," Maggie stammered. Not only had Kelly heard her thoughts, about them learning to fly on their own, but she had blended that with Maggie's memory of Halloween! Impressed, she added, "If we finish cleaning while it's still light, you can go outside and practice."

The girls carried on sweeping with renewed vigor.

By the time Raul came back from town, with two barrels of water, Maggie was ready to assist with the unloading.

Careful to stay where Maggie could keep an eye on them, the girls chose a graded path outside in which to practice with their brooms—she could see them walk up in single file, straddle their brooms, and trot back down in bounding fashion. Up and down they went, while the adults made trip after trip, up the ladder and into the house.

The larger items like the barrels, the mattress and suitcases were brought up by Raul and the workers, while Maggie took care of smaller parcels. It took them no more than an hour and soon Maggie was boiling water in one of the borrowed pots, while Raul moved things around as directed.

The men finished with the steps at dusk and before they left, Arlo announced he would be back in the morning for his regular work— his cousin was not needed for that.

Having set the mattress in the room closest to the kitchen and placing a full bucket of dike water in the bathroom, to refill the toilet tank as needed, Raul also left.

A silent darkness descended upon Maggie and her girls.

Chapter

23

*Sweet Virgin Mary, Angels in Heaven, Holy Trinity,
and all My Ancestors.*

*Thank you for the blessings in my life, most importantly, all
my dear family.
Thank you for your guidance and inspiration.
I entrust my life to you, and I wake up every day,
knowing your wisdom directs what I think, feel, say, and do.
I Thank you, and I Thank the Universe.*

In your name, I pray.

Chapter 23

Maggie flipped a medium sized wooden crate upside down and covered it up with a towel from her suitcase. Kelly set the plastic saucers and spoons on the make-shift table, along with a plate in the center.

Entranced, the three girls watched Maggie as she lit a candle and tipped it. She let the hot wax drip on the plate and when enough of it had pooled, she flipped the candle upright and stuck it on the runny wax.

"Ta-dah!" she sang. "We're ready for our first candlelight dinner!"

A smattering of enthusiastic applause followed the announcement.

Maggie noted, and was pleased to see, her daughters' eyes sparkling in the gloom, seemingly unaware of deprivations. To them, sitting around the table on the swept floor, enjoying soda crackers and the novelty of a bowl of broth with noodles from a chicken bouillon packet, constituted an adventure.

She took comfort in it and tried to put it out of her mind that, besides Arlo sleeping in the storage space beneath them, she and the girls were alone, in the dark, miles from civilization.

"This is pretty," Lizzy made conversation, her voice rising beyond the warm glow of the candle, "the see-through people say we'll do a good job here."

"We haven't already?" Maggie said with a raised brow.

Lizzy didn't reply right away, but after a moment's seeming conference, she said, "Not yet, but we will."

Kelly's eyes flashed from Lizzy to her mother, as if pleading to know what she must make of the conversation.

It won't do to frighten them, Maggie thought, serenely bringing the spoonful of soup to her lips. With a keen eye on her eldest, Maggie contradicted her own earlier thought. "It's nice to know we are not alone here—that we are being looked after."

Kelly relaxed and took another bite of her cracker.

The sudden, overwhelming conviction of her words being true, made Maggie smile. Indeed, there had never been a sense of menace, real or imagined, and on processing that feeling, the light of Maggie's aura, and that of her daughters, amplified the feeble candlelight.

"I think I flew a little bit this afternoon," Kelly chirped excitedly.

"Oh really?" Maggie beamed, glad to see she had managed to avert her distress.

"Me too!" Marie chimed in, making a fist around the broomstick leaning against the crate, "I flew too!"

"No, you didn't!" Lizzy countered. "You were mostly skipping."

"I flew," Marie insisted.

"We were all skipping," Kelly declared, "there were a few times I skipped higher than a regular skip though…" she added, with a dimpled smirk.

"I can fly in my dreams, without a broom!" Lizzy bragged, picking up her bowl and drinking down her soup.

Maggie listened to the youthful chatter of the girls as she slowly ate the thrifty meal. How odd that here she was, supposedly guided by the angels and divine providence, allowing her offspring to indulge in fanciful pagan nonsense.

Possessed by a sudden need to laugh, Maggie squelched the impulse by grinning instead, and saying to Lizzy, "When I fly, I am the green witch. Pray tell, what color are you?"

"Blue," the middle child replied at once.

"Purple! Brown!" Kelly and Marie called out respectively.

Darkness cloaked the hillside home, but light, as if from a dozen chandeliers, spilled out of the kitchen window as the auras of the green witch and her daughters flickered in bright flashes to the rhythm of their chatter.

Although they didn't see them, the stars looked down on their charges and twinkled approvingly.

Having rinsed the dishes and leaving them to dry overnight, Maggie directed the girls to the other side of the wall. She handed each of them a small cup with boiled water that had already cooled off.

"Time to brush our teeth and get into pajamas," she said, placing the candle on the floor so that it could illuminate both spaces. "Kelly, please put a little bit of toothpaste on their brushes."

"Yes, momma."

Maggie pulled out sheets from Nora's bag and began to make the bed. She stretched a thick blanket over it and fluffed the two pillows they'd have to share. She dragged the suitcase closer to the candlelight, the better to look for their pajamas. When she found them, she laid them out on the mattress and the girls, who had finished brushing their teeth, began changing into them.

When Maggie came out of the bathroom, ready for bed herself, the girls were under the covers, giggling and whispering—Lizzy at one end, because she needed to stick one foot out from under the covers or she couldn't sleep, then Kelly and then Marie.

Maggie took her place next to her youngest, and the four witches lay there, staring at the plaster ceiling, oohing and aahing over the dancing patterns of light and shadow created by the flame.

As the chatter slowed, Maggie crossed herself, "In the name of the Father, of the Son, and of the Holy Spirit."

Her daughters' voices joined hers, "Angel of God, my guardian dear, to whom His love commits me here, ever this day be at my side, to light and guard, to rule and guide."

Sleepy 'amens' followed amid yawns, as Maggie blew out the candle, "Sweet dreams, my girls."

"And to you too, momma." Kelly replied.

"How many sleeps until we have our own beds?" Lizzy said through a huge yawn.

"The truck will be here in two more sleeps," Maggie answered, "and tomorrow, we will go through the things that are in storage

downstairs—your great uncle said there was some furniture there we might be able to use."

"Will we have to clean it?" Kelly wondered.

"Of course. But we should be able to handle that in the two days we have until dad and the truck show up."

It was a bit of a letdown that nothing interesting was found in the storage room. Three mismatched weird-smelling wooden nightstands, a rickety work bench that would have to pass for a kitchen table, and a couple of blackened *pailas*.

"They're cookware," Maggie explained, noticing Kelly's puzzled glance at the copper pots.

Nevertheless, under guise of entertaining themselves, Maggie set the task of sweeping the shed while deciding what would remain there. To do that properly, the contents of the shed had to be carried out into the sunlight, only then would they able to attack the walls and low ceiling with their brooms.

"Quit your fussing—the spiders are long gone from those webs!" Maggie chided the girls for being squeamish. She swiped the broom, back and forth, along where the ceiling and wall met. "Grab the broom with both hands, and sweep down, like you mean it!" Maggie said, demonstrating what their portion of the task entailed.

Looking disgruntled, the girls tackled the sooty stone walls, brushing down the ribbons of dusty webs Maggie dislodged for them.

"Our brooms are shorter than yours, and this wall is so long!" Lizzy grumbled.

Kelly didn't comment but exchanged a dismayed glance with her sister—the shed's back wall indeed extended for what seemed an interminable distance.

Maggie wondered if perhaps she was working the girls too hard, but she dismissed the concern right away; this was exactly the type of activity that built character, and in the long run, it was bound to create a sense of ownership and appreciation in them.

"We have today and tomorrow to finish," Maggie soothed, "it does not matter if we do it slow, only that we do it right."

Even Marie let out an audible groan at the news that they would be doing this for two days. Far from entertained, they dragged their brooms carelessly across the wall when they thought Maggie wasn't looking. But for that sort of thing, their mother seemed to have eyes in the back of her head.

The childish craftiness caused an unsettling effect on Maggie. It hinted at the inevitable independence that, once achieved, would rip them from her sphere. How could she delay their stay—extend her influence over them?

Flustered, Maggie began humming a song. Had she acted rashly? Maybe she needn't have come out so soon, after all, a single afternoon had been enough to get their living space ready for the truck's arrival.

We're here though, and I can't turn back time, she thought as she continued to hum, keenly aware that the girls weren't joining in. Maggie looked slantways at them, "Of course, if we do hurry up, we can practice flying in the afternoon!"

It heartened her to see their eyes twinkle in unison.

They'd been up with the sun, so it was no wonder that lunchtime found the shed transformed and clean: dust had been brushed off the garden tools and they now stood against the cobweb free wall nearest to the door. A dozen clay pots in varying sizes were stacked to one side of the tools, ready for when Maggie needed them to plant flowers. Filling the rest of the space were a wheelbarrow, a couple of buckets, a rickety ladder, and an assortment of carpentry tools that Maggie knew would come in handy.

Under the fig tree in front of the house, the girls were wiping down the furniture and cookware before it could be taken upstairs.

"We can have the afternoon off, and tomorrow too!" Kelly cheered, giving the nightstand she had just finished cleaning a couple more smacks with a rag.

Maggie's first impulse was to deny them idle time, but the thought that these were five, three and two-year-old children crept sweetly into her heart. "After flying practice, we will explore until sundown!"

"Yippee!!" cried the girls swinging rags and broomsticks with delight.

"What's for lunch?" Lizzy wondered.

"Well, let's take these things upstairs and I will fix some pâté sandwiches while you wash up."

The girls carried the shiny cookware while Maggie and Arlo, who, at her request, had paused his weeding efforts, carried the larger furniture pieces up the newly repaired stairs.

Maggie directed the girls to wash their hands and faces with the dike water. "Don't let any of it get in your mouth," she admonished them, fretting about parasites while she arranged the nightstands; one in the room they were using, and two in the empty common room. *I'm sure the doctor in town will have a castor oil purge for amoebas.*

Since the wooden crate was no longer needed as a kitchen table, Maggie turned it into a pantry—in it she put all the non-perishables she had purchased at the supermarket. The work bench became their kitchen table, but as they had no chairs yet, they would have to stand around it to eat.

They finished their meal of sandwiches and water, and for dessert, Maggie pulled out chocolate covered cookies from the new pantry. She handed one to each girl.

"Yummy!" cried Lizzy, gobbling up her cookie in two bites. Kelly and Marie prolonged their enjoyment by nibbling daintily on theirs.

With a surge of emotion over the innocent joy such a small treat caused in them, Maggie thanked the angels that her daughters were unaware of poverty or isolation. She took a bite of her own cookie, inwardly uttering the mantra she would repeat every day from then on.

By the time they're old enough to notice any of this, I will have changed it.

Chapter
24

Outside, the equatorial sun shone through patchy clouds, desiccating the land beneath. A mild, dry breeze played with the dust, causing it to dance in lively swirls, that splashed and collapsed against tree trunks, or dispersed into the cool shadow of the alfalfa rows.

In their makeshift kitchen, Maggie wiped down the table where they had eaten. She threw the breadcrumbs out the door, and paused, abruptly reminded of Santa Victoria, where the chickens scratched the dirt for grain beneath the old kitchen.

A sweet memory, to be sure, but Maggie had loftier ambitions, and she had entrusted the angels with the 'how' of it. She meant to search her dreams and look out for signs of their answer so that, one day, instead of a rickety ladder leading up to their kitchen door, there would be a handsome terrace, hung with a sumptuous, magenta Bougainvillea. There would be a birdfeeder, and a proper staircase too!

Beaming at the vision she had conjured, Maggie turned to face the three expectant little girls, already holding their brooms. As promised, after lunch, they went outside and set off on their exploration.

They started up the western slope, along the corn fields and rows of bulb onions, to the main dike lined with Eucalyptus trees. And then, they took their time going back down, to the east end of the property, along the lane dividing them from the large mansion.

The beautifully landscaped grounds, with fruit trees and pines and enclosed gardens, again spoke to Maggie about the caste she had been flung to, among the alfalfa and other lowly crops. She pursed her lips.

"Look, momma, look how pretty!" Kelly hollered, as if bidden to derail her mother's cross thoughts.

Maggie stared broodingly at the flowers Kelly held in her fist, but soon, her expression cleared. She accepted the invitation to turn from notions of having been spurned, to looking at reality through her daughter's eyes.

"See the dainty white petals? And the full yellow tummy?" she said, dropping on one knee next to Kelly.

Lizzy and Marie gathered round to look too.

"This is chamomile," Maggie informed the girls, prompting them to crush the downy green leaves and take a whiff. "Let's take some back home, and we'll make tea tonight."

The girls collected a few stems under Maggie's watchful eye. "Not much is needed—"

"But there's so many of them," Lizzy observed, nevertheless stopping at three of the pot-bellied flowers with their lacy leaves.

"Still, we must not waste."

"Can we have our own flower garden?" Kelly wondered, helping Marie to pinch off a stubborn stem to complete the tiny bouquet, and reminding Maggie of the flower shop in faraway New York.

The balmy, sweet smelling back room that had been her workplace, seemed invented now—if it had ever existed, it was a lifetime away from her arid surroundings now. And yet, everything around Maggie, from trees, to crops, to shrubs and lawns, confirmed the fertility of the land; life-giving water from the dike ensured it.

"I don't see why not," Maggie smiled, seeing beyond the dust in the shimmering afternoon light, "each of you shall have a plot to tend to."

Lizzy's brow knitted, "Is tending hard?"

"Only at first," Maggie laughed, "look, the sun's gone behind the mountain, can you feel the chill in the air?"

"Yes," Marie said taking Maggie's hand as they headed up the lane, back to their coop. Kelly and Lizzy brought up the rear, on their brooms.

"Dark comes quick!" Kelly gasped, and four sets of eyes took in the dense fog tumbling down the mountain.

Maggie picked up the pace, "Better hurry up in case it decides to rain!"

Somewhere on the other side of the mountain there must have been lightning, but Maggie and her girls only heard the thunder.

They made it home, yet for all the darkness and rumbling, the rain didn't come. In time they would get used to the menacing displays and learn that water from the sky could not be reasonably expected until December, January and February.

After a quick dinner of soup from a packet, again, and crackers, they had their chamomile tea.

"It doesn't look very good," Lizzy pulled a face looking in the pot where the stems and flowers were steeping.

Maggie poured the liquid into their cups, masterfully keeping the limp leaves and petals out. Lizzy rejected hers after one sip but was tricked into drinking it after Maggie added one more teaspoon of sugar.

"It tastes just like it smells," Kelly remarked, trying to sound grown up.

"But do you like it? Maggie asked.

Kelly nodded diplomatically, as she finished the contents of her cup.

While they cleared the table, Maggie heated more water on the camping stove. When it started to boil, she shut it off and brought the saucepan with the near-boiling water into the bathroom. She mixed it sparingly with the cold water already in the bathing bucket.

From the door, Lizzy and Marie watched Kelly get a bowl of lukewarm water dumped on her head while doing a frantic rub down.

When her turn came and amid breathless complaints, Lizzy followed Maggie's orders.

"Soap up quickly and scrub all the dirt off!"

"It's s-s-so c-c-cold!" Lizzy said, running the bar of soap hastily over her body.

"Here you go," Maggie dumped another bowl full of water on her, "look at how dusty you were!"

Through chattering teeth, Lizzy laughed at the dirty foam swirling down the drain as she made the best of the last bowl of water being dumped on her.

Maggie wrapped her in a towel. "Dry yourself and go put your pajamas on."

Lizzy shivered out of the bathroom as a buck-naked Marie came in—Kelly was already in her nightshirt and under the covers.

Soon, the four of them were in bed again, staring at the ceiling by candlelight.

"We're getting a surprise tomorrow."

Maggie could hear the smile in Lizzy's voice, so she looked across the mattress, over Marie and Kelly. "Of course, we are. Dad is bringing our truckload of things tomorrow!"

"That too," Lizzy said smugly, causing Maggie to prop herself up on her elbow to inquire farther.

"What else is there?"

"I don't know what else, they just said we will be happy about it."

"The see-through people?" Marie said, gathering the blanket protectively under her chin.

"Yes. White petals are floating everywhere," Lizzy said in a faraway voice.

"Chamomile petals?"

"No. They're bigger ones."

Maggie rested her head on the pillow next to Marie. The littlest witch snuggled closer straightaway. Hadn't she been thinking about gardens earlier, about the flower shop, and about Santa Victoria?

Maggie sighed, *my white, birthday roses.* Could the see-through people, like Kelly, pluck her thoughts right out of the air and whisper them to Lizzy?

"In the name of the Father..."

The girls followed the leader, and on their closing 'amen' Maggie snuffed out the candle.

Looking forward to the commotion the new day would bring, for she longed to arrange her things in the new space and make it look like a home, Maggie grinned in the dark, acknowledging that a hefty dose of excitement was bubbling inside of her, in anticipation of tomorrow's surprise.

Whether it had been imagined or prophesized by Lizzy, Maggie didn't doubt it was on its way.

Chapter
25

Despite there being no east-facing window in her room, Maggie's eyes opened as soon as the curve of sun glimmered in the distant horizon. She indulged in listening to the little girls' peaceful breathing, delaying the moment of fully waking to begin the day.

Angelo won't be here until ten, she thought, *and that's if the truck wasn't delayed*.

With a start, she realized she had no way of knowing if there'd been a change of plans. Taking mental stock of the two days' worth of non-perishables in the kitchen, Maggie shrugged off the concern. Besides, even without the truck, Angelo would come to check on them.

Squinting in the gloom, she checked the glowing hands on her wristwatch; *six-twenty*. Maggie stretched her limbs and yawned, "Just a few more minutes," she whispered, gathering Marie to herself and closing her eyes.

She slipped into a waking dream straightaway.

Over the flower shop there was a wide-gap trellis covered in plastic, beyond which Maggie could see the blue sky. Like a soothing caress, the perfumed air entered her lungs with every breath she took. On a long table strewn with clippers, ribbons, and cellophane, lay nine white roses for a new bouquet. She had already removed their thorns and whatever leaves looked shriveled. "Now, baby's breath," she said, bending to look for it in the buckets under the table, but her chin caught the top of Marie's head, and Maggie woke herself up.

With a jolt, she grabbed the wristwatch. *Eight-thirty!*

"Good morning!" Maggie called, scrambling out of bed. The girls barely stirred. "We overslept, and Dad is almost here!"

That seemed to register with the drowsy children. Kelly and Marie sat up yawning and rubbing their eyes. Lizzy rolled over on her back and stared grumpily at the ceiling.

Maggie came out of the bathroom wearing a sweatshirt and jeans. She tied a bandana over her hair, ready for a day of hard work.

"Everybody up!" she said, pulling clothes out of the suitcase. "Please go potty and get dressed while I fix us some breakfast."

After a quick meal of scrambled eggs, grilled toast, water, and instant coffee for Maggie, they trooped into the bathroom to brush their teeth. They watched Maggie flush the toilet by deftly long-pouring a bucket of water, without sloshing any of it!

"Now it's time to put everything away. And we'll sweep again so the place is clean when the truck arrives!" Maggie announced, pulling the blanket off the mattress and folding it.

"I'll go get our brooms," Kelly said, racing out of the room.

"Lizzy, Marie, please get the sheets and pillowcases off the bed, and afterward we'll stand the mattress up against the wall."

There really wasn't much to it; by the time Kelly came back, the floor had been cleared out and the four of them set off to sweep the rooms, remarking on how much dust had accumulated in two days' time.

Bustling by an east-facing window, Maggie paused on spotting the funnel of dust approaching.

"Dad is coming!" she called to the girls.

They raced over to see for themselves.

"Is he inside the dust?" Marie wondered aloud; her nose pressed to the glass.

"He's in the car, inside the dust," Kelly replied.

It seemed a long time until they were able to make out Raul's truck, followed by a larger one.

They climbed down the kitchen ladder, and went around to the front of the house, just as the first truck pulled in.

Maggie could see Angelo waving gleefully from the passenger seat. Holding Marie on her hip, she waved back.

"It looks like someone is in the back seat," Maggie said to the girls, squinting and shading her eyes to make it out, but the cloud of dust made it impossible.

The moving truck pulled up too. It stopped with a series of clatters near the recently repaired steps.

Angelo jumped out of Raul's truck, his first embrace was for Maggie, and Marie, since the little one was in her arms. Then Kelly and Lizzy.

"Oh, my goodness!" Maggie cried out.

As one, Kelly and Lizzy, who'd been clinging to Angelo, turned to see what the matter was with their mother.

"I can't believe it!"

The third person in Raul's truck was Maggie's brother, Sebastián. He had returned from California a few months before, and unbeknownst to Maggie, Angelo had recruited him to be on standby in anticipation of the ship's arrival at port. Of his own accord, as much as to please Dolores and Vicente, Sebastián accompanied their belongings to his sister's family settle in.

"So good to see you, Maggie!" Sebastián said, giving her a one-armed hug, careful to keep the parcel in his other hand from getting crushed.

The girls gathered around their uncle, greeting him and clamoring for hugs. Sebastián laughed good naturedly and obliged, though he first handed over the parcel wrapped in white plastic to Maggie. "A surprise, from Mother," he winked.

Maggie pulled off the covering and gasped. Tears welled in her eyes as the sultry scent of Santa Victoria soil overwhelmed her. There were four cuttings stuck on the dirt, and Maggie didn't have to ask, she knew her mother's loving hand had cut them from her birthday rose bush.

"What a comforting, inspiring surprise this is," she exclaimed, marveling at the transporting effect a bag of dirt and four cuttings had on her.

She could see herself in a lush garden, walking arm-in-arm with Dolores! But Lizzy's uproarious laughter, as Sebastián threw her up in the air and caught her, quickly brought Maggie back to the dusty sunlight.

This must be the surprise her see-through people foretold. With a smile playing on her lips, Maggie deposited the precious surprise inside one of the pots in the storage shed, safe from the commotion already ensuing.

"There won't be enough daylight hours for what we mean to do," Raul remarked, hands on hips as he eyed his loaded vehicle and the moving truck.

"Then we'll just have to stop time," Maggie laughed.

"You don't know Maggie," Angelo chuckled, "she can organize a tornado and make it do her bidding."

Maggie was indeed in her element.

"There is a place for everything, and everything will be in its place," she said to the able-bodied men. At her request, they walked through the upstairs to familiarize themselves with where their belongings would end up.

She breezed from one end of their house to the other, pointing out locations, "Here is the girls' room… here is our room. This is the living room… and here is the kitchen."

From then on, all Maggie and Angelo had to do was tell the others where unmarked items should go. Even the girls formed part of the moving crew, carrying smaller parcels to the designated spot in their new home.

By mid-afternoon, the moving truck had been emptied out, and the driver had been paid and released. The group had a quick bite before resuming work, relieved that there wasn't much left in Raul's truck.

Ben E. King's, *This Magic Moment*, warbled out of the transistor radio. Maggie hummed along with it as she came into the kitchen with a last box of the things Nora had donated.

At the window, Maggie paused to watch the dense mounds of fog tumbling down the mountain, by now she knew they would dissipate before reaching the house, but she still delighted in their boisterous onset.

"Well, we're all in now," Maggie said under her breath, glancing at the boxes stacked here and there in the darkening interior of their home.

Only beds would be made up that night, to accommodate the family and guests, the rest would get unpacked day by day.

While the men took care of assembling frames and mattresses, Maggie and the girls worked in the kitchen—Angelo had already set up their stove with its propane tank.

Dinner was a lively affair, what with flickering candlelight and so many people sitting around a proper table and chairs! Sebastián regaled them with details about the retrieval of the cargo, its transfer from ship to truck, and the journey after. He relayed all the well wishes and greetings entrusted to him by Dolores and Vicente. All of which were received by Maggie with infinite relish and gratitude.

While the men enjoyed a well-deserved beer, Maggie moved on to locate pillows, sheets, and blankets, and by eleven o'clock that night, they finally made it to bed, exhausted.

Having Angelo by her side gave Maggie a much-needed sense of confidence that all would be well. The few days' separation had softened Maggie's disappointment, allowing her to let go of the hurtful resentment, most of it anyway.

She thought of the rose cuttings on the kitchen windowsill. They didn't look like much—four bags of dirt with a dried up twig sticking

157

out of each one—but Maggie could see what they would become; soon they would produce leaf shoots, meaning the roots had taken hold, and for a blinding moment the symbolic vision took her breath away.

Her life, at present, didn't look like much either, but Maggie knew in her heart that it would bloom, beyond her wildest expectations.

White petals everywhere...

158

Chapter
26

M aggie could not recall a more congenial weekend—they planned, worked, and laughed. They ate, talked, and dreamed too—all of it in such perfect doses as to make her long for it never to end. So, when Sunday afternoon came, seemingly out of nowhere, Maggie struggled with a dark sense of being left behind.

The reality of the men returning to the city, and of her actual daily life beginning on Monday, cooled the warm glow they had created in the previous hours. So, before it was time for them to leave, reacting to her intuition, Maggie stole away with Angelo to a nearby grove where they might talk in private.

"It was wonderful having you here," she confessed, and he gathered her to him in a tight embrace. In his arms, Maggie found the strength she needed to voice her concerns, "Angelo, don't forget about us."

"Not ever!" he said, sealing the promise with a kiss.

Holding tight to one another, they went over their understandings and certainties. Angelo's uncle may not have given them the closed-up manor, but he did give them the rent generated by the land on

which their house stood. Maggie would manage it, and on his death, they would have the title to the property outright.

In Maggie's mind danced schemes to make their land produce crops well beyond alfalfa and corn.

A new highway from the city to their home, was under construction. When completed, Angelo's commute would be shortened by over an hour. But, because that wouldn't happen for several months, Angelo would have to bunk with Nora and Raul and come home on the weekends.

"But I will be able to see Kelly every night and, hopefully, ease her loneliness," he said.

Maggie found her opening to introduce what had been foremost in her mind for days.

Her heart soared when Angelo readily agreed with her plan to hold Kelly back from school.

"I promise you, I will generate the necessary income to purchase my own car, so I can take the girls to and from the nearest school bus stop."

Another kiss, one more embrace, and hand in hand, they walked back to the house.

Uplifted by their talk, Maggie began compiling her to-do list, prioritizing such items as unpacking, planting, laundry, and looking into necessities like electricity, water, and phone service, for which she and the girls would have to walk into town.

It was full dark when Angelo and Sebastián climbed back into Raul's truck. Sebastián would return to Santa Victoria by bus, and Angelo would take him to the station on his way to work.

Chapter 26

Surrounded by her girls, Maggie stood in the truck's headlights, waving goodbye, as they backed out into the road.

They remained there until they could no longer hear the rumble of the engine, and the hush of the waning moon settled upon them.

"Did someone take a bite off of it?" Lizzy wondered, staring up at the sky.

Maggie laughed, "It sure looks that way."

"It makes me dizzy to look at it—why is the moon moving so fast?" Kelly said, holding on to the belt loop on Maggie's jeans to steady herself.

"It's not the moon that's moving fast, it's the clouds," Maggie explained, "there must be a lot of wind up there."

Since Raul had left the transistor radio behind, Maggie didn't hesitate to turn it on to liven up their candlelit dinner and the tidying up afterward.

Through the windows, the twinkling stars followed Maggie and her candle, from one bed to the next, as she kissed the girls goodnight.

"A place for everyone and everyone in their place," she whispered, leaving the common room to the tune of rustling sheets, creaking box springs, and a sleepy string of words uttered by Lizzy, surely to her see-through people.

From her bed, under the window, Maggie stared at the stars and yawned. "When the new moon comes, I will transplant the cuttings to their own pots."

A rather pagan scheme threaded itself into her thoughts, why not nestle each root in a lock of hair?

In the mysterious starlit silence, Maggie reflected upon it. Had Dolores sent four cuttings in case some did not take?

No. Of course not! It's one for each of us; for me; for Kelly; for Lizzy; and for Marie.

She stretched and grinned, hailing the whole as an inspired idea. All was right with the world. "Here is where we put down our roots."

The stars twinkled in the serene heavens.

Chapter
27

In the budding household, the four days until the new moon did not go idly by.

First thing on Monday morning, Maggie enlisted Arlo's assistance for a trip into town; he was as decent an attendant as could be hoped for, and he had a donkey, which Maggie felt would come in handy on the way back, when the girls might be too tired to walk.

All of Maggie's stops in town were either on, or near, the main square. With Arlo's help, she located and pleaded her case for water, and utilities at each office.

Satisfied with the responses she got; Maggie splurged for a treat at a small shop boasting homemade blackberry and soursop ice cream.

They sat on a park bench—Arlo on the grass—to savor them.

"I like chocolate better," Lizzy frowned, barely touching the blackberry ice cream with the tip of her tongue.

"I'll eat it if you don't want it," Marie piped up, she was almost finished with hers.

Lizzy seemed to consider finishing it, as opposed to sharing it. "Well, hurry up then!" she said in the end, holding the cone away from her as it had begun to melt. She let it drip onto the pavers while Marie shoved every bit of her own cone in her mouth. Lizzy handed hers over, looking disgruntled. "Next time I want chocolate."

"I don't think they have that flavor," Maggie warned, "since it's homemade, they must use only the fruit they can get around here."

"No chocolate?" Lizzy said, aghast.

"Maybe in other stores?" Kelly offered.

"There is another store by the convent, all they sell is ice cream," Arlo informed them.

"Excellent! Thank you, Arlo. Next time we come into town we will check there."

"Can we go there now?"

"No, Miss Lizzy, we need to head back home while you all have the energy to get up the hill," Maggie replied, feeling a pang of sadness for Lizzy. Any homemade ice cream here would be a far cry from the tasty five cent Thrifty cones they used to buy in California.

"Do we get to ride the donkey?"

"Yes, Marie, but once we get out of town and across the main road."

"I don't want to ride the donkey," Kelly fretted.

"I don't *need* to ride the donkey," Lizzy asserted.

When they reached the beginning of their lane, Maggie's knowing glance passed over her girls. If she could feel the equatorial sun beating on the top of her head, so could the little ones. The glare of daylight caused her to squint, and the dusty air stirred up a thirst that, she knew, could not be slaked until they reached home, three quarters of a mile away.

"Well, here we go. Last push," Maggie said.

They had laughed and skipped on the way down the steep slope, but now, Lizzy groaned as they started up it.

"I wanna ride the donkey," Marie announced. Lizzy frowned at her.

Arlo stopped and pulled the animal to him by the lead rope. He petted his forehead and withers, holding him steady while Maggie perched Marie, side-saddle, on the donkey's bare back.

"You hold on to the crest, right here," Maggie instructed.

"It's twitchy."

"It is, but you need to hold on anyway because there are no reigns or saddle, and I don't want you to fall off."

Marie continued to squirm, holding tight to the mane, seemingly unable to find a comfortable spot on the donkey's spine.

Arlo clicked his tongue and they were off again.

The slope leveled as they took a right turn. Soon they would be inside the tree tunnel.

"I want to get down now."

Arlo stopped and drew the donkey close again, while Maggie scooped up Marie and put her on the ground. "Do you two want to try it?"

Kelly and Lizzy exchanged a shifty glance—eyes bright on flushed, sweaty faces—they bobbed their heads in unison. Maggie perched Kelly on the donkey, both of her legs hanging on the right, and then she scooped Lizzy up on the left side.

"Kelly, hold on to the crest, here. And Lizzy, you link your arm to Kelly's."

"I shouldn't hold on to the tail?"

Maggie squinted at Lizzy. "No!"

"His hair is prickly," Lizzy complained as soon as they set off, "and his spine is hard," she went on, making a show of rearranging herself atop the patient animal.

"Hold still," hissed Kelly. She had positioned both buttocks on one side of the spine while her upper body leaned forward to compensate. "I don't want to fall off!"

A few yards later, obviously having had enough, Lizzy let go of Kelly's arm and flung herself off. The sudden move spooked the donkey, causing it to buck awkwardly.

Maggie lunged, "Lizzy!"

Kelly yelped and grabbed a fistful of mane to steady herself. Arlo yanked the lead rope, forcing the donkey to submit.

"What!" Lizzy, who had toppled onto her knees, stood up and dusted herself off, "I didn't want to ride anymore."

"Next time, say so, and I'll help you. You could've hurt yourself or made your sister fall!"

"I don't need help," Lizzy muttered under her breath.

"Well, we're almost home, just a little bit longer," Maggie said, unsettled by the lapse in judgment. How did she not foresee there would be scrapes, or, God forbid, broken bones to handle in this far-flung outpost? She didn't even have a first aid kit!

She stared at Lizzy, plowing on ahead, kicking the fine dust as she went. How would that child fare in the world with her attitude of do first, then think?

This weekend, when Angelo comes back, we'll go into town and get a basic first aid kit, Maggie promised herself.

She gave Marie a piggyback ride the rest of the way. "Just think, girls, before we know it, we'll have running water, a phone line, and electricity!"

"But I like the candles at night." Marie pouted.

"Don't fret about it. We'll always have candles and we'll be sure to use them every now and then."

The rest of the afternoon was spent going through boxes and trunks.

Peeking over her mother's shoulder at the open chest, packed tight with sheets and towels, Lizzy flared her nostrils.

"Is this what it smelled like where we were before?"

Maggie closed her eyes, pressing a mint-green bath towel to her nose. "Yes. It's different than here, isn't it?"

Marie scooted over on the floor to take a whiff too, "Why, momma?"

"I think it's because of the laundry detergent we used, and also because the air smelled different," Maggie said, brushing the long bangs away from Marie's eyes.

Lizzy wrinkled her nose. "It's dusty, and it smells like smoke all the time here."

Kelly, who had been looking out the bedroom window, casting a suspicious eye on the tumbling fog, sniffed a couple of times and whispered, "Why are they always burning stuff?"

"Well, the laborers work all day to clear the fields. They pile up the weeds and then they burn them slowly," Maggie said, shutting the lid to lock in the scent a little longer. Maybe, memories of their other life in the sun and ocean breeze, could be kept fresh too.

In a distant voice, she continued, "Their adobe huts in the hills have wood-burning stoves to cook on, and to keep them warm at night. Since they burn all day and all night, they're always sending smoke up in the air."

Now it had been brought up, Maggie couldn't help smelling smoke on her clothes and skin. But, as nothing could be done about it, she must move on to the next thing.

Since their bedrooms were not equipped with closets, there really wasn't a point to unpacking. Maggie decided to assign a trunk or a suitcase to each of the girls, to serve as dressers, until real ones could be built or bought.

Back in the kitchen, Maggie tackled the pots, pans, dishes, and silverware currently strewn on the lone countertop beneath the windows. She organized them all in boxes, on the shelf beneath it.

The refrigerator became the pantry, "This will have to do until we have electricity," she told the girls, directing them to transfer all their non-perishables into it.

Besides Angelo's fashionable *Radiola*, the living room had no other furniture. They would have to wait to furnish it, but in the meantime, Maggie stacked boxes there to create the illusion of spaciousness in the bedrooms.

In the evenings, after dinner, they listened to two songs on the radio, to save the battery. Then, they watched the low-hanging stars through the window until Maggie announced it was bedtime.

On that Thursday night though, Maggie lingered by the window, remembering that Kelly had remarked multiple times on how the moon seemed to grow smaller and smaller every night.

From one of the boxes in the living room, Maggie pulled out the Farmer's Almanac.

"It's a cycle that never stops," Maggie said, opening the booklet to show them the illustrations of the lunar phases and their names. "Tomorrow is the New Moon, so tomorrow we'll transplant the rose cuttings."

"Why?" Marie scooted closer, the better to see.

"Your *abuelita* Dolores always says that the new moon imprints everything with the energy of a new beginning."

"And we are at the very beginning," Kelly said, her little girl voice thick with wonder.

Maggie kissed her forehead, elated afresh to have spared Kelly, and herself, the trauma of premature separation.

Chapter
28

They spent Friday preparing for the ritual planting of the four rose cuttings. Maggie filled four clay pots with a mixture of manure and soil from their new home.

Wide-eyed, like little owls perched on a branch, the girls watched her aerate the soil and then make a hole in the middle.

"OK. Each of you, grab a pot," Maggie instructed, picking up her own pot and a pitcher with water. "We'll take them to the back patio and let them sit there, under the open sky, until dark."

"It smells funny," Marie wrinkled her nose.

"It's the manure."

"Will our roses smell like that?" Kelly wondered.

Maggie laughed, "I used to wonder the same thing when I was your age."

"Were your roses smelly?"

"No, Miss Lizzy, and these won't be smelly either."

When the fog bounded over the mountaintop and began to tumble downhill, like a mute frothy wave, Maggie decided the time had come. She handed a cutting from the windowsill to each girl, she grabbed her scissors, and they headed outside.

"Although we can't see it, the new moon is there, watching us," Maggie told the girls, setting down her cutting and scissors.

Marie cast a nervous glance up to the sky, "Can it really see us?"

"Mmhm. But it's not a scary thing," Maggie soothed, "its powerful force can produce a whole new life, that's why we are planting our roses tonight, and that's why we're putting a bit of ourselves into the pot too, to see what kind of magic comes from it."

"What little bit of us?" Lizzy quipped, her glittering eyes on the scissors.

"Only a tiny ringlet of your hair," Maggie smiled.

"Oh."

"Are we ready then?" Maggie asked, grinning at their intuitive choices. The girls had lined up just as they had on the big mattress, before their beds were delivered. Lizzy had claimed the pot at the far end, followed by Kelly's, and then Marie's, which was snuggled up to Maggie's.

She directed them to sit on the ground, opposite her, with their pots in front of them.

"We'll do this oldest to youngest."

Modeling for the girls, Maggie grabbed a lock of her own hair, clipped it about a half inch from her fingertips, and placed it in the hole on the dirt. "You next, Kelly."

The cool breeze, the quick snip of the shears, and the gooseflesh on bare arms, gave the scene a veiled sense of ritual, as Maggie reached from one girl to the next.

"Now, take your cutting, and peel off the plastic bag—like this—do it over the pot."

Three silent nods followed each new instruction, Lizzy's accompanied by a distracted, "Mmhm."

"Mind the thorns," Maggie admonished as they handled the green cuttings, which had already developed a tiny root ball. "See how it's holding tight to the Santa Victoria soil?"

More silent nodding while avoiding the thorns.

"Now let's put them in their new pots, right on top of the hair you just put in there. And now, firm the dirt around it, like this, so the cutting stands tall."

"Will we have roses next week?" Marie asked, focused on piling, and patting down the dirt around it.

"It will take a lot longer, maybe three or four years," Maggie said in a resigned voice.

Kelly paused mid-planting, "Won't the new moon speed up the growing?"

Hearing the challenge in Kelly's voice, a fanciful memory struck Maggie, prompting her reply.

"These do come from my magical rosebush in Santa Victoria, so yes, with the help of the new moon, and if we sing to them, they may end up blooming in one!"

Lizzy looked up from her work, rubbing the dirt off her hands. "A whole year?"

"It's better than four," Kelly rallied; eyes trained on her cutting as she tested the firmness of the dirt around it by trying to tip it.

"Well," Lizzy rejoined airily, "mine won't be white though, my hair will make my roses blue."

"Is that so?" Maggie looked at her daughter with a raised brow, "I thought the see-through people told you there would be white petals everywhere."

"They did because your roses will be white, but mine will be blue."

"I think mine will be purple," Kelly joined in.

"Mine will be daisies," Marie asserted in all seriousness, causing Kelly and Lizzy to burst out laughing.

What madness is this? Maggie shuddered, staring at the three girls in front of her, again feeling them as separate entities from her. And although it made her heart ache, it also amused her that her daughters' individuality kept catching her off guard.

Gathering the discarded bags, she began humming one of her favorite flower songs. After a few bars, Kelly picked up the tune and soon all four of them were humming along and giggling over the improvised changes to the words they knew; *every morning you meet me... small and purple... clean and blue....*

Maggie glanced up at the sky with giddy anticipation—the new moon's powerful energy whispered to her that Lizzy's blue roses would come, so would Kelly's purple ones.

And why not, Marie's daisies, and Edelweiss too!

Maggie ran her household much like Dolores had in Santa Victoria, where everyone had jobs for every day of the week. By Maggie's design, there should never be an idle moment. That included napping at around four in the afternoon—a task Maggie had imposed on herself—so she could deliver a strong finish of the day.

Since she didn't require the girls to nap, their assigned task was to tend to the rose cuttings, singing while they sprinkled them with water.

Three days from the planting ceremony, while Maggie napped, they went down to check.

Lizzy gave her cutting a tentative tug, "Ah!"

Kelly and Marie paused, mid watering, to see what the matter was.

"My root is holding on—good and tight. Try yours!"

The girls went upstairs to report the exciting news of slight resistance. They stood at the edge of Maggie's bed, whispering.

"Poke her on the shoulder."

"You do it. She'll get mad at me."

"Marie, you do it!"

Maggie rolled away from them.

Kelly clicked her tongue. "Momma, the cuttings are holding on!"

Maggie smiled sleepily, trying to place herself in the moment, but the dream she'd been having seemed to cling on. The girls' chatter faded—the balmy air of an indoor garden overwhelmed her senses for a moment—somewhere far away Lizzy tried to talk over Marie while Kelly shushed her. But Maggie couldn't focus, when had she been in that garden?

As the girls' voice broke through the luscious foliage and the thick perfume of the flowers, Maggie opened her eyes, dazed.

"Oh," Maggie yawned and stretched, "did I hear correctly? Is our rose garden taking hold?"

"Yes, momma, the roses and my daisies are coming!"

Brushing Marie's bangs from her eyes, Maggie smiled at her daughters. She had never been in any such dream garden, but she would be—they all would—just as soon as she created it.

Already there were four plants to start it off!

Chapter
29

With the highway construction not yet completed, Angelo continued to board with his sister, Monday through Thursday. He came home every weekend, ready to address Maggie's never-ending honey-do list.

"There is so much I want to do," Maggie said one Friday night, stacking the dishes after dinner, "I have to figure out how to get an extra six hours in every day."

Angelo laughed, "Thank you for dinner, that was wonderful."

"Foremost in my mind, is getting that second car, so we can get the girls to school." Maggie pursed her lips, mulling over the best way to tell him of the strange vision she'd had, and which had triggered her growing fixation about a garden.

"I'm really pleased with how the rose cuttings from Santa Victoria are doing," she said, piling the dinner plates into the kitchen sink. "Soon we'll need to move them to a more permanent location."

"Should we designate a plot for a flower garden in the back?" Angelo offered.

"Well, I was thinking of something more than a plot, maybe a greenhouse—or something like that."

"Oh."

Maggie's heart beat faster as words poured out of her, feeding the image in her mind, amplifying it and giving it intricate detail.

Angelo nodded eagerly, as if swept up by the idea, "We can start out with a small structure—I can build it myself! And it will be expandable for whatever comes later. With the weather being so mild here, we can certainly start out with a plastic covering, but eventually it will be glass."

Tears of joy sparkled in Maggie's eyes, every last trace of disappointment in her husband, vanished at his demonstration of solidarity. "Maybe part glass, and part wooden pergola?"

"And stone pavers, and fountains!"

"Benches, and gravel walkways!"

"What is it called?" Angelo said, eyes aglow, as he reached for her hand.

Maggie laced her fingers with his and said, "Jardines LunaRosa."

From that moment on, Maggie's life sped up as if the placid Doldrums had puffed her over to the spirited Trade Winds.

First thing on Saturday, they sought out the town carpenter. Maggie, Angelo and the girls staked off the square footage designated for the future site of Jardines LunaRosa. How grand it sounded!

On Sunday, they covered the dining room table with page after page of penciled plans for each phase of the project. Raring to roll

it out, Maggie found it hard to sleep that night, lamenting that the weekend had flown by with nowhere near a level of progress to suit her eagerness.

At the crack of dawn on Monday, Angelo headed back to his sister's, to start the new work week. In her robe and slippers, Maggie waved goodbye, thinking of her own busy days ahead.

In his absence, a supernatural magic seemed to favor the blossoming household in the shape of new leaves.

Before the frame for the temporary greenhouse was even assembled, the Santa Victoria cuttings had begun to sprout! With a shudder of excitement and disbelief, Maggie observed the differences Marie's stalk exhibited.

"I'll be damned," she muttered, hands on her hips. It had started out like the others, with protrusions like thorns dotting the stalk, but the new moon and Marie's hair—maybe even the little girl's pronouncement— had caused the shoot to change until it became greener, and the protrusions smoothed out but for a couple of budding leaves.

Encouraged to buoyancy and taking a leaf from her daughters' book, Maggie made up her mind to expect blue and purple roses.

"Our LunaRosa really is enchanted!" she declared triumphantly. "Girls, fetch us some lemons from the tree down the lane, we're making a cake to celebrate!"

With every passing day, convinced of the mystical alignment she had happened upon, Maggie asserted authority in her new home. She executed well thought out decisions with confidence and persisted wherever results were not up to her standards.

Owing to her tenacity with the town council, it took only three months to get running water, electricity, and a hand-crank telephone installed in their dining room.

It was decided that Jardines LunaRosa would begin at the center of the rectangular plot. Angelo and the carpenter put up a basic wooden pergola there, three sides of it and the roof were lined with plastic. The first residents of that space were the four Santa Victoria cuttings, which Maggie and the girls had already transferred into larger clay pots. They would remain there until their final location came into existence.

Maggie called in a favor to her angels, and she cut a deal with the moon too, so that all the phases of the garden might be completed in two years.

Although Jardines LunaRosa was not expected to yield roses in that first year, Marie's daisies sprouting so enthusiastically brought Maggie a wonderful idea.

The new moon once again witnessed a ritual; the little girls stood under the pergola, like sentinels posted at three of its corners, shielding the flickering light of their candles with a cupped hand. Four clay figurines: Mary and three angels—one of them was Raphael—Maggie had informed the girls, kept a watchful eye. The wheelbarrow in the center held a large mound of compost, Maggie's own concoction of organic fertilizer.

That night, they traded their brooms for shovels and rakes to mix the smelly, magical fertilizer on the newly turned soil along the perimeter of the pergola.

"And now," Maggie said, leaning on her rake, "we let this sit overnight, for the stars, the new moon, and Mary and the angels to watch over."

"Are we planting tomorrow night?" Kelly said, wiping her forehead with the back of her hand.

"No-no. First thing in the morning, so the seeds and bulbs will soak up all the night magic before the sun hits them."

"We have to get up before the sun is up?"

"Yes, Miss Lizzy. So, tomorrow might be the day you take a nap."

"I'm not a baby, I don't need a nap."

"Tell us again the names of the flowers and tell me which ones are the ones I get on my flowerbed," Marie chirped.

"We all get sweet peas, daylilies and lupines, but at the center of each flowerbed, there'll be something different. Kelly has lavender, Lizzy gets her snapdragons, Marie gets the sunflowers. And I'll have dahlias."

While they waited for plants to grow and flowers to bloom, Maggie set out to establish contacts in town that might eventually sell their bouquets. She also put her girls to work making square tags out of brown cardboard. Each one bore a single water-color image; Kelly made hearts, Lizzy made stars, Marie made daisies. Maggie inspected each for quality before writing on the back, in beautiful calligraphy, "Jardines LunaRosa." The last touch was a hole punched on a corner, so that the personalized tag could be tied to each bouquet.

Under the watchful eye of Mary, the angels, the moon and the stars, they cheered, month after month, for every new bud and shoot.

As a family, they had scoped out market days, and had made themselves known in their small town. And it was with starry-eyed excitement that they prepared their first arrangements.

Angelo drove them into town and waited in the car while Maggie transacted business.

The forewarned store owners smiled kindly on her, and although she felt they could have done more to showcase her wares, Maggie saw no point in telling them how to run their business.

She didn't want the tags to get wet, so she dumped two thirds of the water from her assigned bucket before placing three bouquets in each one. She told the shopkeeper the price at which they were to be sold and went off to repeat the same process at the other two stores.

The family spent the rest of the morning walking around the square, browsing the fruit and produce stands, and greeting acquaintances.

Maggie's heart leapt to her throat when she spotted one of her bouquets in the hands of a lady, who could be heard from across a produce aisle, making too low of an offer on a dozen eggs.

"Oh my! Look, look!" Maggie said out of the corner of her mouth. "We've sold one!" She could hardly contain her excitement.

"That was one of mine," Marie whispered—she never missed a detail.

"How do you know?" Lizzy said, incredulous.

Wagging her head, Marie smirked, "I saw the daisy on the tag."

Maggie steered them all toward the shops, anxious to check how many more might had sold.

"Oh, my goodness!" she breathed, squeezing Angelo's arm, "there are none left here—let's go check the other two!"

By the time vendors in the marketplace started to pack up their displays, all nine bouquets had been sold.

"As inaugural offerings go, this has been a complete success!" Angelo sang out the last two words, beaming at his wife.

"Soon, we'll be an all-season supplier. Soon, we will have our own outlet in the market!" Maggie rejoiced.

"I will deliver flowers on my broom, all the way to California," Lizzy said, "and I will get paid in chocolate ice cream."

They all laughed at this, but Maggie's brow furrowed—she hadn't thought about the brooms in a long time.

The sudden recollection of that moonless night, her little girls holding candles under the vigilant glance of Mary and the angels, tickled her funny bone. With an impish grin on her face, Maggie wondered if they minded coexisting in the garden with her little pagans.

She laughed out loud, picturing pointed hats on Mary and the angels, and quickly crossed herself.

Chapter
30

Flowers bloomed in Jardines LunaRosa as bountiful as the notions in Maggie's head. No sooner had she conceived of them than they flowered into exuberant existence.

The highway was completed, and a honeymoon feeling took over Maggie—what a treat to have Angelo at home every night!

She set up her own vending space at the weekend market and in no time, Saturday mornings and Sunday afternoons—after mass—were devoted to the flowers. Religious icons, even if clad in witch hats, might withhold their blessings otherwise.

They grew so much in popularity that Maggie, consistently, sold out within an hour from the market starting.

"It takes you longer to set them up than to sell them!" Angelo remarked as they loaded empty buckets back into the car.

"One of these days I'm going to have my own flower shop, like the one I used to work at in New York."

"Oh, I'm sure it will be even better than that!"

If anyone in the household felt they couldn't keep up, Maggie's jet stream would sweep them up and carry them. Her energy was as inspiring as it was irritating to some in the household, especially those who might have appreciated more leisure time. But even they could not deny Maggie's penchant for achieving results.

When she had saved enough money to purchase a used truck from an acquaintance in town, Angelo began her driving lessons in earnest. As with everything else, Maggie seemed to pluck an instinct for it from thin air. Soon, she was venturing into town on the weekend, by herself or with the girls, while Angelo worked around the house.

The new acquisition also signaled that the time had come to have a conversation with Kelly and Lizzy. Maggie had delayed it for over a year, but there were no more excuses now, the girls would start school at the beginning of September.

In the couple of months before that came to pass, along with the Santa Victoria white roses, came the exotic purple and the blue. Egged on by the overwhelming evidence of magical powers, which in Maggie's mind equated to cosmic assurances of success, she pulled out the old plans to expand and complete Jardines LunaRosa.

With minor revisions, a timeline was set for the expansion.

Having inquired about the school bus route, Maggie loaded up the girls into her pickup truck one day and took them for a practice run to the bus stop.

A wide-eyed Marie stared at her sisters, seeming to fear for them. "I'm glad I don't have to go yet," she squeaked, snuggling closer to Maggie.

Marie's comment apparently resonated with Kelly, who squirmed and gazed at the empty sidewalk across the street. "Other girls will be there to take the bus with us, right?"

"Yes, they will. But you won't have to wait there alone. I'll be here until the bus comes."

Maggie's assurance seemed to calm Kelly's spirits, and she even smiled a little when Lizzy piped up.

"I've never ridden a bus before."

Maggie could tell that the exciting changes in and around the household were barely enough to distract Kelly and Lizzy from the looming unknown. She had never told them about her own somber experience at school, so her girls had no idea what a nun was. Besides attending mass on Sundays, where they mixed with natives and landowners on crowded pews, they had no notion of religious rituals.

A school run by nuns would be an adjustment, to be sure, but Maggie believed it was the best education she could offer her girls and, most importantly, it was within their limited budget.

Maggie's second excursion into the city, driving herself and the girls, was for the purpose of giving them a tour of the school. While there, they would also stop at the procurement room to purchase their uniforms.

With eyes trained on the road ahead, and more to herself than to Kelly and Lizzy, Maggie said, "You are old enough to make up your own minds, and whether you like a situation or you don't, you must adapt for the best."

On the bench seat next to her, the girls said nothing.

Experiencing a flutter of discomfort, Maggie wondered how they would handle the fact that Kelly was a year older than her first-grade classmates, and Lizzy, a year younger than other kindergarteners.

They're old enough to learn to make the best of things, Maggie thought, ignoring a fleeting impulse to tell them herself about this peculiarity. But how could she explain about the circumstances that prevented them from starting at the mandated time? Or the even more puzzling premonition she'd had, about Kelly staying at Nora's.

Maggie took their silence as a sign of their internalizing what they'd seen and heard. She chose to let them be.

During the drive and on entering the mammoth schoolhouse with its chapel, Maggie noted the effort it took for them to keep their reactions in check. Kelly shrank in the seat, while Lizzy squared her shoulders or, at times, leaned close to Kelly to mutter something Maggie couldn't hear.

Marie seemed petrified by her surroundings and would not let go of Maggie's hand.

There was no lively chatter on the drive back home, so Maggie started humming and then outright singing. But the girls kept to themselves.

Nothing was said until a couple of days later, when Maggie caught Kelly staring uneasily at the stiff, navy-blue pleated skirt and collared white shirt hanging in the closet.

"You are excited to start school," Maggie said, hoping to alchemize Kelly's anxiety by pretending to see an opposite sensation.

Kelly looked up, startled. Tears welled in her eyes, making it seem as if they were emitting sparks. She nodded and Maggie recognized a little girl trying to be brave.

"It is a really big place," Kelly squeaked, blinking away the tears.

"The more room to explore," Maggie suggested, hopefully.

Kelly nodded again. "How will we know where to go?"

"No need to worry about that. The bus pulls right into the parking lot where the ground floor patio is. That is where the morning assembly happens every day."

"That's the place that has the Snack Bar at one end?"

"That's the one. And since you're going into the first grade, you don't need to worry about the second floor, because that is for seventh graders and up. And on the third floor are the nuns and the girls who live at the school."

"They're boarders, right?"

"Right."

"But we will take the bus back to the stop, every day, and you'll pick us up, right?"

"Right." Maggie gathered Kelly to her and gave her a tight hug.

Unlike her older sister, Lizzy seemed to be looking forward to wearing the new, austere outfit. Despite Maggie's entreaties that she must not get it dirty, Lizzy had taken to wearing the sailor's collar flap, stressing that, "I like how it snaps into a tie, like dad's."

Shaking her head, Maggie threw up her hands. But Marie's voice came from behind her mother, to needle her sister, "You won't be able to wear different color socks anymore, especially with your uniform and a dirty collar flap."

Maggie laughed out loud at the observation. Lizzy's bend for wearing mismatched everythings would certainly suffer when it came to the school uniform.

Lizzy held her tongue, content to glare at both of them.

When the laughter dimmed though, Maggie wondered what would happen with Lizzy. Once the excitement of the unknown wore out, she was bound to realize how tedious school could be, especially for someone with the wrong temperament. And Lizzy was as ill-disposed to regulations as a child could be.

From that perspective, perhaps it was the nuns Maggie should worry about!

With that in mind, and to redirect Lizzy's unruliness as much as to spare Kelly from brooding, Maggie reacted to a sudden pagan impulse.

She pulled out the final drawing for LunaRosa and laid it on the dining room table, determined to syphon their energies away from uncertain speculation and into a single, positive vision!

"Kelly, please get the watercolor case and brushes. Lizzy and Marie, bring four cups with water."

Curious, the girls did their mother's bidding and gathered around the table, expectantly.

Maggie lit a candle and set it on the windowsill.

"Close your eyes," she told them.

In a singsong voice, running her finger over the drawing, Maggie imagined and called to their minds all the features planned for the garden: its ponds, walkways, benches, roses, ferns and more.

"Can you see our LunaRosa? Smell the flowers, hear the water trickling, and the gravel crunching underfoot. Do you see it? ...And now that it's finished, open your eyes."

The girls blinked in the candlelight, their glance falling on the penciled sketch.

"Let's color it!" Kelly bounced in her chair.

"Yes! Let's turn it into the enchanted garden it's going to be," Maggie smiled, satisfied.

Chapter
31

LunaRosa's original pergola became a full-blown greenhouse with a glass dome. It housed a café, complete with kitchen and workshop.

As each phase of the garden came into its full splendor, Maggie and Angelo hosted a proper inauguration—a fitting opportunity to invite the lively, ever-growing circle of friends and family, to infuse the garden with their positive vibrations.

The four cuttings from Santa Victoria, practically unrecognizable in the sumptuous plants they had become, adorned the four corners of the greenhouse. The history of the white, purple and blue roses, and Marie's daisies, was well-known among their acquaintance, who considered it the stuff of legend. It also gave Jardines LunaRosa its lucrative mystique.

Opposite the entrance to the greenhouse, across the brick floor, sat a fountain with waterfall. Angelo, who had left his job in the city to devote his time and creativity for a larger, more meaningful return at home, had designed a dual waterway, with a pump hidden behind the fountain, to allow waterflow to either side of the garden. The two brooks flowed in opposite directions from the fountain: meandering along gravel paths and mounds of assorted ground cover, before returning to the source, by way of an underground pipe.

Benches strewn along the way, invited visitors to pause and admire the luscious clutters of lilies, tulips, lilac bushes, and peonies.

Iron arches, hung with flowering climbers, separated sumptuous vistas of colorful hydrangea bushes, bursts of baby's breath and wallflowers, and camelias and orchids, nestled among thriving ferns.

Amid that dazzling beauty, on a warm Saturday afternoon, seven-year-old Lizzy had lined up four hummingbird feeders—Maggie had asked her to refill them.

The breeze carried the music, from the festivities in the greenhouse, to all the winding gravel paths. It reached her where she worked among the lilac bushes.

She heard the footfalls on the gravel and turned to see who it was.

A man, a friend of her parents', had evidently strayed from the party.

He sidled between the fragrant flowers to get closer to her. "What are you doing?"

Although prepared to be polite—like she had been taught—Lizzy froze as the usual murmur of the see-through people intensified in her head. She answered them, "But, I have to refill the feeders."

Lizzy thought she heard the man say, "I don't see any hummingbirds." She wanted to tell him they wouldn't come until the feeders were refilled, but she didn't.

"Later," the see-through people pressed, so insistently that Lizzy couldn't hear anything but their voices. "Look at the sky, Lizzy, look at the cotton clouds—let's fly up there!"

Her belly tickled with excitement—how she loved to fly!

"Ok," said the little girl, and she left with the see-through people, not caring that the man was standing way too close to her, or that he had grazed her cheek with his sweaty fingers.

"Momma."

Maggie rolled over groggily. Even in the dark room—it couldn't be more than two or three in the morning—she could tell Lizzy was standing just inches away. "What is it?"

"Momma, I peed in my underwear," she sobbed.

Maggie sprung out of bed, bewildered by the unlikely incident. "Oh? Let's get you to the bathroom then."

She took a sniffling Lizzy by the hand and guided her in the dark, their feet padding softly on the floorboards.

She flipped the light on.

Blinking away the momentary blindness, Maggie adopted a matter-of-fact tone, to hide her confusion as much as to convey a sense of security to her distressed daughter.

"Do you need to pee a little bit more?" she asked, helping her out of the wet panties.

Nodding, Lizzy climbed on the toilet, while Maggie inspected the underwear with a sinking feeling that soon turned to rage. The color and consistency, the faint lingering smell!

Sweet virgin Mary.

"Not to worry, my Lizzy," Maggie whispered, kissing the top of Lizzy's head, even as her mind reeled with speculations. Yet by sight and expression, the child was convinced she had only peed in her bed!

"Not to worry," she repeated herself, "accidents like this happen all the time."

"Has it happened to you?" Lizzy whimpered.

No! Maggie's mind screamed as she scooped up the little girl from the toilet and put her in the tub.

"It happens to everyone, but then we grow out of it." She ran the water through the handheld sprayer, "Let's get you cleaned up, and back into bed."

Oblivious to Maggie's turmoil, a comforted Lizzy climbed into bed.

"G'night, momma," she yawned.

At the door of the girls' room, Maggie had to pause on hearing Kelly begin to whisper.

"Lizzy—"

"Mmhm?"

"I saw you fly over the garden earlier."

Through another huge yawn, Lizzy whispered back, "I went the highest ever!"

"I didn't believe you before—that you could fly—but now I do."

"The see-through people came for me when I was supposed to be filling the birdfeeders."

Astonished, Maggie turned slowly toward the small voices. Her glance passed over Marie's bed. With a shudder, she saw the tiny glint of her eyes, opened wide and listening to her sisters.

"Time to go to sleep, my sweet girls," Maggie whispered and at once, mattresses creaked with girls rolling over and resting their heads on pillows. She left the room not knowing what to make of what she'd heard, but certain that she must get to the bottom of it.

On Monday morning, Angelo took Kelly and Marie to the bus stop, while Maggie took Lizzy to a pediatrician in the city.

How she wished they could have found a female doctor, but as it was a pointless hope, Maggie had to overcome her distrust.

Holding the doctor's scrutinizing gaze, Maggie explained that there had been over thirty guests at the gathering that weekend. For the life of her, she couldn't think who might have done such a thing.

"I understand," said the doctor, turning to Lizzy with a kindly expression. "Let's have a look at you, young lady."

Lizzy glanced at Maggie as if asking for permission. She gave her a reassuring smile, "I'm right here with you."

There was no avoiding the examination, so Maggie held Lizzy's hand and spoke to her for the whole two minutes it lasted.

The doctor set her down from the exam table and sent her behind the privacy screen so she could change into her clothes again.

"There is a discharge of unmistakable nature," the doctor said gravely.

The tears welled up quick. Maggie wiped them off with the back of her hand, nodding briskly.

"Oddly," he continued, "she doesn't seem to know what happened."

Lizzy came out with her clothes back on, mismatched shoes and all, just as she liked. If she understood any of the carefully exchanged words, she gave no sign.

Maggie thanked the doctor, "I will keep an eye on her, and let you know if there are any developments."

She took Lizzy's hand and led her out of the doctor's office, relieved though more perplexed than ever by the incident.

"How about we go to the craft market, you and me?"

"Yes!" Lizzy beamed, "and can we have lunch there? And dessert?"

"Yes! And then we will surprise Kelly and Marie. We'll pick them up when school is out, so they don't have to ride the bus today."

After lunch, sitting on a bench at the square, enjoying the afternoon sun, mother and daughter ate their chocolate ice cream.

"Lizzy, what did you mean when you said the other night, that you had flown the highest ever?"

"It was the see-through people, momma, I didn't finish filling the birdfeeders because they took me flying when that man came to see what I was doing."

A sinister chill descended on Maggie. "What man? What did he look like?"

"He was tall, and sunburned. He had hair like mine, only darker."

Images of the guests shuffled like cards on a deck in Maggie's mind, until *yes! The wretch!* He had even patted Lizzy on the head when he and his father arrived! "This is my son; he is visiting from Argentina," he had said.

Maggie's last bite of ice cream came back to the top of her throat, but she took a deep breath to stop it.

"Are we about ready to go get your sisters?"

"Mmhm."

Chapter
32

M aggie had not expanded on the reason why, so Angelo never suspected there was anything untoward about one of the girls needing to see a doctor.

When he returned home, she did not breathe a word of the confirmed incident to him because the inevitability of what she meant to do, forbade it.

Not for Mary, or the angels, this task.

Those men would never, ever, be invited to her home again, that went without saying. As for the scoundrel himself...

On the first night of the full moon, after the girls had gone to bed and Angelo had immersed himself in a movie, Maggie went to the greenhouse.

Petals and leaves glistened in the bluish moonlight; the balmy, perfumed air caressed her. Her slippers padded softly on the brick floor of the café's kitchen. She opened the top drawer of the workbench, grabbed a wedge of *palo santo* and dropped it into the pocket of her quilted robe, where there already was

a matchbook. She picked up four candles, and a serrated stem cutter too.

"Come to me," she called to Lizzy's see-through people, certain that although she had never seen or heard them before, they would heed her summons on this night.

Come to me. She meandered on the gravel path to the place where it happened. *Come to me.*

With an aching heart, she spotted the forgotten feeders, lined up, just as Lizzy had left them.

Maggie took the stem cutter and poked a hole in the dirt, in front of each one, and buried the candles halfway.

"I thank you for sparing my child from the horror that happened here," she said in a taut voice, lighting candles, one after the other. She lit the tip of the palo santo next and blew it out after a few seconds.

The fragrant smoke billowed around Maggie, competing with the faint scent of lilacs. "It cannot be undone, I know, but it must be avenged." The four flames flickered in unison, the tip of the palo santo glowed brighter, giving Maggie momentary pause.

Do I really want to do this? She pressed her lips together in concentration. *Yes. I cannot call myself a mother if I don't.*

"Let him know no peace," she exhorted the see-through people, "not until he has lost what he values as much as I value my daughter's innocence."

In reply, the see-through people snuffed out the candles. Maggie's heart thumped in her chest, marking the seconds as they passed.

Chapter 32

The smoldering tip of the palo santo throbbed and dimmed in the silence, until it too stopped.

"I will not take it back," she muttered, rising from her crouching position. She grabbed the feeders, refilled them, and hung them back from their iron spikes.

As she walked back home, the moonlight diluted any remaining doubts, "I've done nothing but quicken a wave of karma."

With that relieving conviction, Maggie released herself from further reckoning on that score. She never bothered to follow up and so never learned that what the scoundrel had valued most had been his health and vitality. He lost them both, within a month of Maggie's fateful visit to the garden, inexplicably and with the force of a lightning bolt, never to enjoy them again, for as long as he lived.

The distressing ordeal had caught Maggie so off guard, that she only had a mind to focus on Lizzy's immediate well-being and bringing about karmic justice. Maggie deemed Kelly's claim—to have seen her sister fly—a less urgent matter, which was soon dismissed as fancy, and eventually forgotten.

She thanked the see-through people, and every star in the sky, for saving Lizzy's mind and spirit from the ravages of the act. Her middle child knew nothing of it, as Maggie had daily proof.

Kelly, being the little radar that she was, had not only seen Lizzy fly, but had witnessed what her sister had been spared. She recorded the incident in her nine-year-old mind, so distinctly, that in time, Kelly came to believe it had happened to her, more than to Lizzy, who didn't remember any of it, apart from the flight.

Chapter
33

By Maggie's design, Jardines LunaRosa became the family's flagship enterprise. From selling bouquets at the local market they grew to distributing their famed flowers all over the country.

In five years' time they had managed to buy the land from Angelo's uncle. They also acquired several neighboring plots, which Maggie and Angelo put to good use by creating a citadel of sorts. It had its own entrance and she soon turned it into a beautifully forested location. One half of that property included the nine villas where the garden's employees and their families lived.

Rows of Pepper trees lined the cobblestoned entrance to the citadel and divided the villas from the garden with its circular driveway and parking area.

Jardines LunaRosa thrived, indeed, yet no amount of hard work, success or recognition could ever diminish Maggie's devotion to family. Since the long-ago day in New York, when she realized that her parents and siblings came before all else, Maggie's heart had expanded to include Angelo's family too.

She became a soothing balm to their old resentments. Perplexed as she had been by them, Maggie found ways to infiltrate and mend their relationships, determined to teach her own girls to cultivate love and harmony in their lives as well.

Their ample means allowed Maggie to establish strict traditions aimed at sustaining a powerful family network—she saw herself as the ruling matriarch, and her home could not be otherwise but the network's motherhouse.

The family bought in to Maggie's scheme, and their collective calendar burst with plans: summer vacations were spent either at the coast, where Angelo had materialized his dream of building a beach cottage, or abroad, with Maggie's sisters, the merry-god-witches. Christmases found the party of five with Dolores and Vicente, where the girls could understand their roots and bond with that entire branch of the family. The other holidays were spent locally, at home, or with Angelo's family, for the same reasons.

Be it parties, barbeques, or road trips, the Moretti family calendar was always full. But, as life will sometimes have it, turbulence struck one evening in September, seven years into the stabilized life Maggie had created.

She and Angelo attended a party in the city, hosted by Raul's employer. Maggie dazzled in a green tunic, and Angelo made a striking figure in black. They entered the smokey cocktail lounge where clusters of people chatted and laughed, sipping drinks while puffing on cigarettes.

Raul beckoned them to him and Nora, and Maggie and Angelo joined their circle for the required introductions.

Angelo took a champagne flute from a passing waiter and asked for water too, as Maggie never drank. The waiter nodded and left Maggie with a momentarily clear view across the room.

Time stopped and then warped backwards. Through the cloud of smoke, Maggie saw him.

From yards away, Alonzo reached into her heart and unlocked the chest she had shut tight years before. He grabbed the stack of letters she kept there and questioned her with gleaming eyes.

Taken aback by the unexpected vision, Maggie stumbled over memories, *I burned them*, she thought frantically, but Alonzo would not quit her. The waiter returned with her water, blocking him from her line of sight.

"Thank you," she dismissed him, taking the glass, and seeking Alonzo out again, but he had vanished.

In vain she moved from one cluster of people to another, hoping to catch a glimpse, but after a fruitless hour Maggie had to conclude he had left.

Angelo came to her as the crowd began to funnel into the banquet room for dinner, "Is something wrong?"

Maggie hardly knew how to answer. She could not decipher what was in her heart and her mind was in such disarray that, as they found their table and took their seats, all she could do was blurt out a half-truth.

"I feel like I've just seen one of Lizzy's see-through people."

"That's disconcerting," Angelo remarked, "do you think the girls are ok at home?"

"They're not toddlers anymore, and Iris is there, she knows where to reach us if something happened."

"We'll call them after dinner," Angelo said, and Maggie agreed, filled with remorse.

Angelo's take on her statement made it so she would not be able to revisit the incident and explain it to him. She would have to keep the unsettling glimpse of the past all to herself.

Maggie liked that and gave herself permission to put the incident out of her mind for the rest of the evening.

Not until they were back home, well past the witching hour, while Angelo snored blissfully beside her, did Maggie breakdown the intense exchange and its effects on her.

She had known all along that Alonzo lived in the city and still she had failed to prepare a response in the event of an encounter. A sad oversight, but now that the unexpected had happened, Maggie counted herself lucky to have avoided a verbal exchange. The shock of the meeting would have kept her from acting natural, and that would have been regretful indeed.

Nearly ten years had passed since their last communication, yet in the few seconds she had seen him, Maggie managed to glean a sense of his wellbeing, surely he had a family of his own and he appeared successful, in whatever his endeavors might be.

The fact is our brief history in common does not compare and cannot change what we have built separately.

With that final thought, which she would repeat to Alonzo if ever she ran into him, Maggie threw the letters back in the empty chest. She slammed the lid shut, once and for all, rolled over onto her side and fell asleep, exhausted.

Sweet Virgin Mary, Angels in Heaven, Holy Trinity,
My Ancestors and My Sisterhood.

Thank you for all the blessings in my life.
Thank you for your daily guidance and inspiration.
Most importantly, thank you for this new day,
in which everything I think, feel, say and do,
manifests love, light, health, harmony, and abundance
in my life, and the lives of those I love.
I Thank you, and I Thank the Universe
I Thank the Moon and the Stars

In your name, I pray.

Chapter

34

firm believer in taking opportunities as they come, Maggie gave herself license to intervene when she could be of help, especially where it concerned the family.

When things got tough for Nora, after she and Raul divorced, and it became evident that the self-proclaimed socialite, who hadn't worked a day in her life, was having a breakdown, Maggie averted the drama with a trademark practical suggestion.

So it was, that the face cream Nora and her sister made at home, for their personal use, became the first of a successful skin care line, made and sold exclusively at Jardines LunaRosa.

Angelo had engineered the workshop to optimize the flow of steps, from trimming and assembling bouquets, to packaging them for distribution. He had no trouble adapting it to accommodate production of the skin care line, which soon bred flower infused soaps, lotions, and toners.

Nora tapped into her newfound talent for marketing and luckily, she had a social circle large enough to provide for her income needs.

As it was in the beginning, Maggie's girls oversaw the labeling for all their products, but on entering their late teens, their attention dispersed in following their own pursuits.

Like LunaRosa, Kelly, Lizzy and Marie had come into their own. The required revolutions around the sun had seen them through elementary and high school, and while no one was as good as Maggie at setting expectations, she could not deny that something had gone amiss with her own daughters in that area.

Well, with one of them, the most pressing case at the moment.

To Maggie's chagrin, either on purpose, or by being perfectly oblivious to what would please her mother, Lizzy wrote notebook after notebook, filled with baffling pagan stories she claimed were whispered to her by the see-through people.

With a doubtful raised brow, Maggie had bit her tongue as it became clearer and clearer that Lizzy meant to become the clan's chronicler.

While Kelly and Marie discussed and embarked on their higher education, Lizzy curled her lip at it.

"Mom, I won't load up my brain with stuff I don't want or need!"

Angelo laughed heartily at this, and even agreed with their middle child. "You're ahead of your time," he would say, wincing in good humor when Maggie's eyes flashed disapproval.

"As early as Kindergarten I knew that discipline and academic achievement were not for her," Maggie bewailed the point to Angelo in private. "She says the see-through people have become her advisory committee. Angelo, our frowniest child is out of her mind! And you approve of her holding council with them instead of with us, her living kin?!"

Angelo shrugged and grinned, which only made her feel alone in her fears for their prodigal child.

When Kelly completed her general education courses and decided her career path would be holistic Psychology, Maggie threw up her arms, defeated. It never occurred to her that Kelly's unexpected calling might have a direct link to Lizzy's forgotten flight from the garden.

"Why are these two so averse to profitable occupations? Why can't they be more like Marie, who's decided she'll one day become a professor! Have I not set up a good enough example for their success?" Maggie railed.

"Why on earth would Kelly and Lizzy not be successful in their chosen pursuits?" Angelo asked in all seriousness.

The reminiscent tone of the question silenced Maggie—no point trying to make an ally of him in this cause, after all, she alone knew what was good for her girls.

Despite her exact calculations and expectations, the three girls flew the coop pell-mell, to test the wings their mother had given them. A solemn-looking Maggie had sent them off, each time repeating to herself that children are but borrowed treasures, and that fearing for them would be nothing short of distrusting the very upbringing she had provided.

Nevertheless, Maggie's powerful blessings chased her daughters wherever they ventured, from Kelly's home in the city, to Lizzy and Marie's in California. With a pang of jealousy, Maggie thought of Lizzy reuniting with her lilac bush, which Olivia had faithfully kept all those years.

Although she understood that the family network continued to expand, Maggie resented that it was at the expense of tenants in the motherhouse.

Now those three extensions of herself had left her orbit, Maggie had no choice but to perfect her supernatural reach. She previewed the girls' struggles in her dreams, which inevitably triggered the lighting of numerous candles first thing in the morning, followed by a harried phone call to the distressed child.

"It's a good thing you only pick up distress signals," Lizzy laughed on the other end of the line one morning, but Maggie could tell something was wrong.

"I knew it! What distress? What's wrong?"

"Nothing is wrong, mother. I just got another rejection—I'm supposed to get a lot of those before I get my literary break."

In the young woman's voice Maggie could hear the stubborn little girl, who would have her way no matter the obstacles.

"Well. It won't be the last, as you often say. I'm glad you have proper employment, though, while you shoot for this dream of yours."

After a heavy pause, she heard her daughter sigh.

"That's right, so no worries, mom."

They exchanged a few more words, mostly highlights about family members, and then they hung up. Far from soothing her, the call left Maggie feeling restless.

She tried to inject her day with a business-as-usual feeling, but to no avail, until an unexpected distraction came.

"It is a near impossible feat to try to plan a surprise for you," Angelo said while they had lunch, alone in their kitchen.

Maggie looked up from her salad, "What?"

"Yes. Your fiftieth birthday is less than a month away, and I wanted to throw a surprise party, but that is impossible, as we both live and work here."

Maggie smiled sheepishly, her worry over whatever distress Lizzy might be facing, left her, as she reached across the table and squeezed Angelo's hand. "Thank you! It's the thought that counts."

For as long as she could remember, Maggie had looked forward to her birthdays with undisguised relish. She had certainly considered throwing a party herself, but this was so much better.

And maybe, nothing besides the latest rejection was wrong with Lizzy after all—Maggie's anxiousness was nothing more than her subconscious mind moping over the fact that two of her daughters would not be with her to celebrate the milestone birthday.

The four-course dinner, expertly executed by one of Maggie's tried-and-true caterers, and the subsequent party would be in the glass domed atrium of Jardines LunaRosa.

The cocktail hour began at seven o'clock, amid verdant foliage bedecked with winking faery lights. Cheerful guests filed in, their glances shifting from the bewitching birthday lady to the glittering, lush surroundings.

Near eight o'clock, when it seemed the last of their guests had arrived and the banquet might begin, Maggie caught sight of a van pulling up on the circular driveway. Grasping Angelo's elbow, she called his attention to it, as the driver came around and rolled open the door.

"Oh, my goodness!" Maggie exclaimed, clutching the star-pendant necklace with one hand while with the other, she squeezed her husband's arm.

It transpired, that for all his talk of impossibility, Angelo managed to surprise his wife after all.

A beaming Vicente and Dolores descended from the van, and after them came Kelly and her steady beau.

Breathless, Maggie left her husband's side to embrace her parents.

"What a lovely, lovely surprise!" she cried, overwhelmed.

"Happy Birthday, my Maggie," Dolores said, kissing her daughter's cheek.

Through the tears of joy welling in her eyes, Maggie saw movement behind a radiant Kelly.

"No, it cannot be!" she screamed.

"Mom! Happy Birthday!" Lizzy and Marie called out as they bounded toward her.

"Oh! This is too much! How can this be?" she cried, opening her arms to her two girls as applause erupted behind them.

Reminded of her audience, Maggie whirled to face them, arms hooked tight to Lizzy and Marie on either side of her. She felt like a celebrated actress accepting an unexpected but well-deserved award.

The banquet, which should have started at eight, was delayed until the new arrivals were greeted and introduced, but soon enough people were seated, and the delectable courses began to appear on the tables.

The entire night had a dream like quality for Maggie. "My heart can't take this—so much happiness! It almost feels like something bad is bound to follow it," she whispered to Angelo sometime near midnight, her glance passing greedily over her daughters and parents.

"Don't do that," Angelo whispered back, "bliss is not a perpetual state, so it's moments like this that give us strength to deal with the others."

"I love you," she murmured, kissing him on the cheek as he guided her to the dance floor, for the first notes of a *bandoneón* had signaled the beginning of a Tango.

The couple took the floor to a new round of applause, started by their daughters, and loud calls of ¡*Qué viva la santa*!

By four o'clock in the morning the last of their guests left, still intoning gleeful toasts to the health of the birthday girl.

Kelly's beau had gone back to the city near two in the morning. Dolores and Vicente had retired to the house at around the same time.

After closing the gardens, the family of five walked back home, at an easy, exhausted pace.

"LunaRosa has definitely been christened into a second calling," Marie yawned.

Maggie yawned in reply, "What do you mean?"

"This is a perfect location for receptions, mom. We should put our heads together and come up with pricing packages to accommodate birthdays, anniversaries—"

Angelo opened the kitchen door for them, and the tired ladies filed in. Lizzy bringing up the rear.

"Anybody want some tea before we go to bed?"

"Not for me, my sweet, Kelly," Angelo said, kissing her on the forehead, "I'm going to bed."

"Goodnight, dad," Kelly replied, setting the kettle on the stove. The others' blown kisses and wishes for sweet dreams followed him out of the kitchen.

Marie got the cups and saucers, Lizzy the napkins and limes, and then they joined their mother at the table.

"What are you all smirking about?" Maggie said, looking from one girl to the next.

"Marie's got a good point," Lizzy grinned, "about the garden, that is."

"Oh?"

"Yes! But not just birthdays and anniversaries—weddings too."

"Oh, sweet virgin Mary!" Maggie's hand flew to her forehead, "What are you saying to me?"

It all came out between giggles, stifled squeals, and the whistling kettle. Their respective relationships had taken a serious turn, and over nearly a year of comparing notes, the three of them kept arriving at the fanciful idea of a tri-wedding, in Jardines LunaRosa.

"After all, this is where our *hairy* roots are," Lizzy laughed.

Maggie pursed her lips and glared at her middle child but could not be upset—not really. She shook her head at all of them, for the other two would not stop laughing.

Having settled that the tri-wedding would be in September, and with the sun already brightening the eastern sky, they finally went to bed.

Seven months hence, wedding bells would ring!

Chapter 35

events could not have unfolded more to Maggie's liking. Though there were some concerns, on Angelo's part, about Lizzy and Marie's fiancés, the flurry of planning and documenting had begun.

"The girls' wedding will be our test-run for implementing Marie's idea," Maggie said, tapping her chin with a pencil as she flipped through the pages of a pad covered in notes and ciphers.

"Naturally. But are we sure about these men we haven't met?" Angelo brooded.

"It's not like they appeared out of nowhere," Maggie retorted, looking up from her notepad, "the girls have known them these past two years, at least—and my sisters in California have nothing bad to say about them," she added, as if that settled the matter.

Angelo clicked his tongue, "I suppose you are right."

"What is this really about?"

"I guess, losing the girls to marriage feels like a more permanent loss than them traveling, or choosing to live so far away from us."

Maggie set down her pencil. She put her arms around her husband and kissed him. With a playful smile she added, "How about if instead of looking at this as 'losing the girls' we look at it as how much closer we are to getting grandchildren!"

"There is no derailing you once you make up your mind," he said, eyes twinkling, "still, it's disconcerting to think we will meet them on the same day I have to give my daughters to them."

"True," Maggie frowned, "but think about the fact that my parents didn't meet you until after we were married and had children. Neither did your mother, God rest her soul."

Angelo seemed ready to argue the point, but Maggie interjected, "We can only assume our parents felt what you are feeling now, but even if we had irrefutable proof that they were distressed over our plans, would we have stopped?"

He shook his head.

"I trust these girls I—we—raised, they know where their happiness is. We have to trust their choice."

Either because Angelo changed his mind about it, or because he had no intention of arguing with his wife, the subject was not broached again after that.

The months flew by.

The end of August and the arrival of the California couples, and their respective entourages, was upon them.

For the fortnight the wedding parties would be in town, Maggie had seen to their hotel accommodations, transportation, formal meetings among family members, and sightseeing tours.

The unknown fiancés impressed themselves favorably on Angelo, erasing any straggling concerns he had. Maggie heaved a sigh of relief on that account because, although she would never admit it to him, she had faithfully prayed and lit candles for it to happen that way.

In short, her efforts paid off and all parties were pleased on meeting one another. Her planning skills—which hadn't given her a moment's pause nor required the lighting of any candles—had passed the test with flying colors.

Kelly, being the one most at hand, assisted wherever possible, and when Lizzy and Marie arrived, she couldn't resist joining her sisters back at home, to indulge in Maggie's desired symbolism.

"We will give our daughters away from the home they grew up in."

So it was that, for fourteen whole days before the big event, the family of five was together again, in a house that was a far cry from the dilapidated fixer-upper they had been relegated to years before.

They attended to last minute details and joined in family gatherings with the soon-to-be-in-laws. Their time at home was spent reminiscing and going over the business plan for the expansion of LunaRosa into a private event venue.

The tri-wedding reception would be the inaugural event, with the garden filled to its capacity of one hundred and fifty.

The Catholic ceremony would be conducted at the girls' old school chapel, after which, the motorcade would follow the wedding party to Jardines LunaRosa.

The conundrum of walking the three girls down the aisle was resolved on the day of the wedding, by dispensing with tradition.

"Just this once," Maggie conceded.

She and Angelo led the procession, hand in hand, followed by Kelly, Lizzy, and then Marie.

Something in Maggie stirred at that moment; a furious sense of pride for her part in raising the independent women marching down the path, unaided, to embrace their lives.

Each bride received Maggie's blessing, and a kiss on the forehead from their father, before taking the few remaining steps to her groom.

They made quite a show of sisterhood with their identical bouquets with white, purple and blue roses and daisies, in a nest of baby's breath and leatherleaf fern. It was the gowns though, that whispered sweet everythings about the individual women wearing them: an altruistic romantic, a peculiar mermaid, and a practical princess.

The luncheon and reception at LunaRosa lasted well into the evening.

As with anything Maggie had a hand in, the adjustments to extend the duration of the festivities were smoothed over so that, besides her and Angelo, no one became aware of the efforts.

The music flowed, along with food and drink, until the last guest departed, well after the newlyweds had been transported to their hotel suites near the airport.

Chapter
36

The success of the tri-wedding enveloped Maggie in the cheerful, lingering daze of well-deserved praise. But, as if to confirm her belief that too much satisfaction must come at a price, Libra crept into the astral plane to tip the scales.

Unbeknownst to her honey-mooning girls, Maggie underwent an emergency hysterectomy three days after the tri-wedding.

Fortunately, Dolores and Vicente were still in town to provide comfort and help Angelo as Maggie began the slow recovery. During those long restful weeks, she often mused to Dolores about her womb being gone, the one that had been home to her three girls, to which Dolores always replied, "But so are they, daughter, they have flown the coop."

Recover she did, and as Maggie's energy levels returned, so did the will to infuse Jardines LunaRosa with a new facet in its dynamic life.

She kicked off the marketing campaign, shrewdly returning to old school directories, knowing full well that her daughters' classmates were of marrying age. Maggie wasn't wrong in that assumption, and soon the garden was booked every Saturday for the foreseeable future.

218

"Do you think we should open our schedule to Friday nights as well?" Maggie asked Angelo one afternoon.

"Do we need the revenue?" he countered.

"It's settled then," she smiled, "no sense overloading ourselves."

On the third year after the tri-wedding, Kelly broke the news that she was expecting.

Whether because Kelly was Maggie's first born and it seemed right she should bear the first grandchild, or because, of her three daughters, she was the one nearest at hand, Maggie relished the sense of a cosmic approval having been granted. The universe had signed off on the new life entering the planet!

She lit a candle every day for the safe arrival of the new baby, and when the little girl did come into the world, she pierced Maggie's heart as no one before, or afterward, had managed, not even Kelly's second child, a boy.

In between those two joyous arrivals, there were sorrowful departures as well. Dolores and Vicente, died. Then Emilia, Lizzy's own merry-god-witch, was tragically taken from the family's bosom. They never met Lizzy's girl and boy, or Marie's two girls.

The next orbital shift in Maggie's life, came when, after the death of Kelly's father-in-law, she and her young family had to leave their home in the city.

"They have all scattered now," Angelo complained one afternoon, "I will sorely miss seeing them every week."

Next to him, on the bench swing hanging from the fig tree, Maggie let out a mournful sigh. "It is as it should be. Kelly's place is with her husband and children."

With the reminiscent words still hanging in the air, Maggie wondered how in the world she had ever conceived of children being borrowed treasures.

My girls and my grandbabies are mine, and they should be with me, always!

Having the means and the will, she began organizing yearly visits, either she went to them or they came to her, the point being, Maggie saw her kids as often as she could.

A couple of decades passed in the feverish excitement of planning summer visits; enjoying each other's company for the two to four weeks such holidays lasted; reminiscing for weeks on end about the good times had by all; and then closing the circuit, by kicking off plans for the next holiday.

As Maggie and Angelo got on in years, it became evident that Angelo's more sedentary lifestyle was catching up with him. He detested hospitals and seemingly bent on vexing Maggie, he refused to see a doctor. His yearly flu shot was administered at a local pharmacy, and beyond that, he wanted nothing to do with 'quacks.'

All in all, Maggie could not dress up a persistent sense of foreboding.

"I can't pin it down," she fumed one morning—Angelo had had another rough night. "You've been battling this cold for weeks now. If you don't go to the doctor, I'm going to bring one to see you, here at home!"

He shrugged. "I'm doing better now. A couple more days with lots of vitamin C and this will be behind me."

Maggie looked at him slantwise, "I guess… you don't sound as stuffed up." She walked over to him and felt his forehead, "No fever," she announced, plopping herself down on a chair across from him.

He cleared his throat noisily, "What is it you can't pin down?"

"Something's brewing out there, with the girls, and I wish I knew what it is."

Maggie's premonition became clear a few weeks later.

Both her and Angelo were hit hard when Lizzy, after twenty-two years of marriage, warned them that a divorce was imminent.

Angelo's classic strategy for dealing with things was to speak his piece and release himself from prolonged anxiety. His remarks on the occasion were on point, "You know my original opinion of him was that he was immature, and although he did grow on me over the years, I won't lie. Now I feel betrayed, as Lizzy must, by his infidelity."

For Maggie, the wound was to her pride; to have the stain of divorce on her daughter! Why, it would bring into question the Catholic upbringing she had provided. Didn't that middle child of hers know that Catholics don't divorce?

An irrational desire to sweep it all under rug overtook her. It became imperative to straighten out that willful girl—infidelity was no cause to break up a family!

"He is a good man who made a mistake. He doesn't hit you, he doesn't do drugs, he's not a drunk."

The silence at the other end of the line spoke volumes, which Maggie was quick to interpret—*Lizzy is seeing the light, she's going to think*

better of making an impetuous decision, she's going to place due value on her vows.

As was often the case with Maggie, once on the rampage, she would not back down. Oblivious to the hurt she was inflicting, by diminishing her daughter's experience, she believed that her words had been sanctioned by Mary and the angels. So, when Lizzy spoke at last, Maggie couldn't help feeling blindsided.

"How do I say this without disrespecting you, mom," Lizzy began in a placating tone, "whatever your experience and your faith, I won't submit to a vow that keeps me tied to a man who doesn't love or respect me. And I won't make my kids suffer a day-to-day life where their parents don't love each other. Not for the sake of appearances, and certainly not to maintain a marriage vow that clearly has no meaning to one of us."

Stung, obstinately choosing to see her daughter as she wanted rather than as Lizzy was, Maggie lashed out, "Be reasonable, Lizzy. I did not raise a quitter! And what do you mean 'my' religion—you are a Catholic too, and you must own that you had a heavy hand in this failure. If you hadn't prioritized literary pursuits over your husband we would not be at this crossroad, would we? Nothing but your pride has been hurt so far. You can make amends."

"I'm not like you, mother," came the shaky reply, whose scalding resonance made Maggie wince. "I don't share your matrimonial ideals. You may have raised me Catholic, but you left an open door, out of the convent and into the garden in the moonlight. And the wisdom in that garden is older than yours, or even your Mother Superior's faith!"

"That may be so," Maggie rejoined, disconcerted, "but to go and file for divorce, just like that?"

"It hasn't been 'just like that' it's been coming on for a few months now, and I will not seek reconciliation after a confirmed betrayal—I cannot stomach it."

"Lizzy!"

"Mom, I may have been the one who filed for divorce, but it was only a formality on my part—he's been divorced from me for months. Can you understand that?"

A cursory exchange followed Lizzy's declaration and Maggie hung up the phone.

Disappointed, she blew out the candle meant to illuminate the conversation. If a fear of God and holy vows didn't work on Lizzy, then there really was no turning the situation around.

Sweet Mary, mother of God!

The news of Maggie's daughter getting a divorce would begin to spread among family and their general acquaintance. She must gain control of the narrative to head off criticism!

Maggie made phone calls to key members of their family to introduce a subject that, until that moment, had been discussed strictly between her and her three daughters.

She had braced herself for the worst, so she was caught off guard by people's unexpected reactions, starting with Angelo. No one blamed Lizzy, and no one considered Maggie to be tainted by association.

Maggie realized she stood alone in defending traditions that modern society had given legal remedy to. She heard herself again, telling Lizzy that only her pride had been hurt by a cheating husband, and she couldn't help wincing. Lizzy could have easily retorted, only 'your'

pride has been hurt by a non-traditional daughter, and she would have been right!

Concluding she had been let off the hook from partaking in Lizzy's disgraceful divorce, Maggie assuaged her remaining concerns in the certainty that, with the marriage door closing for Lizzy, surely the windows of responsibility were opening.

Lizzy must be on track to, once and for all, drop the trifling literary aspirations and focus wholeheartedly on her corporate career.

"As a single parent of two, Lizzy cannot do otherwise."

Chapter
37

Two years went smoothly by without a single financial worry, regarding the girls, to cloud Maggie's sky. And thank goodness for that, as Angelo's health seemed to deteriorate daily.

It began with evident lapses in memory; he would insist, bewildered, that new episodes of their favorite nighttime soap were reruns; or he rolled his eyes when Maggie commented on a topic he believed had already been discussed; on a weekly basis he forgot where things went and, on not finding them, he accused poor Iris of having thrown them out.

At her wits' end, and because Angelo refused to go to a hospital for tests, Maggie persuaded a good friend and Neurologist to do a house call. He obliged and after some questioning and a basic check of Angelo's vitals, the doctor confirmed her fears.

"He is otherwise healthy as a horse, but I do believe we're looking at the beginning stages of dementia or Alzheimer's."

The somber prognosis triggered rounds of phone calls between Maggie and her daughters, and Maggie and her sisters. With the former, she discussed what life would be like with an ailing father.

With the latter, she discussed the loss of a partner and source of emotional support.

After fifty years of marriage, here was a hit Maggie had not anticipated. On reasoning through the circumstances, inwardly and with the women in her life, she did not know how to feel about her thwarted expectations.

"We were supposed to grow old together, in full possession of our faculties, in a retirement community, where we would die together, and be buried, side-by-side, in the plot we already bought—following a proper Catholic service," she vented to Nora, who was quick to point out that given the prognosis, her brother's ailment might be a drawn out one.

In truth, at seventy-five years of age, Maggie had come to feel an alien vulnerability. She resented Angelo for relinquishing his share of the responsibility and for openly placing her in charge. But no sooner would the bitterness of the plight bubble up that Maggie quelled it with self-reproach.

"For God's sake! It's not like he's chosen this for himself."

Despite their annual flu shots, Angelo had been catching something during every rainy season. At the end of 2013, a perfect storm of respiratory issues touched down, adding to his worsening mental discomforts. He had begun to realize something wasn't right in his mind, which awakened Maggie and the girls to a deep sorrow, for the inevitable loss looming in the horizon.

The flu became a lingering cold, the cold became a persistent case of pneumonia that stayed with him through long months with little respite. He complained of body aches and spent most of his days in bed.

With a justified sense of urgency, the girls began traveling from California, even Kelly lived there now, to help Maggie and to spend time with their father.

They had already decided that, as his mental condition worsened beyond their capabilities, it would be necessary to move him to an assisted living situation. For the time being, colds and pneumonia could certainly be handled by them. In other words, the four women were emotionally and physically prepared for Angelo's protracted descent into the grave.

Quarterly visits began in March with Kelly and her two kids; in July it was Lizzy and her two; and Marie and her two girls flew in the first part of August.

With heavy hearts they saw for themselves that, while his mental state declined reassuringly slow, the pneumonia seemed a merciless aggressor. Marie and her girls returned home for the new school year, deeply troubled by what they had seen.

On the evening of Thursday the fourth of September, his condition worsened to the point Maggie had to call in an ambulance. She phoned the girls not only to inform them of the urgent intervention, but to thin out some of her distress.

She—Maggie—had caused her husband to be forcibly strapped to a gurney and get hauled off, bellowing. She had followed the ambulance to the hospital, her thoughts in complete disarray.

At the intensive care unit, they injected him with a sedative and antibiotics. As he began to wind down, the medical staff assured Maggie that a battery of tests would be conducted to get to the bottom of the situation.

"Don't leave me," Angelo pleaded groggily, over and over, filling Maggie's heart with remorse.

The doctor tried to ease her mind, "He'll be asleep soon and, anyway, you won't be allowed in the room while we work on him. You really should go home and try to get some rest."

Maggie nodded, sniffling and dabbing her eyes with a crumpled tissue. No point telling the doctor that a sleepless night awaited, with her husband's desperate pleas echoing in her mind.

"We will call you first thing in the morning to let you know how he spent the night," a nurse said, patting Maggie on the shoulder.

Back at home, she urged her girls to delay traveling until she heard from the doctor. Maggie did her best to convey to them that, as upsetting as it had been getting him to the hospital, there was a sense of relief that at long last he was there and in capable hands. Perhaps the lingering pneumonia would become history, once and for all.

Sunup brought no comfort. Maggie held the phone to her ear for a full minute after the caller hung up. Angelo had not survived the night.

A near hysterical Maggie, unable to reach Kelly, communicated to Lizzy and Marie the unexpected news of their father's death. Marie in turn, let their mother know that despite her instructions to delay, Kelly had booked the early morning flight.

"She'll be there tonight, mom, and we'll get there tomorrow," they assured her before they hung up.

Even with an assembly of siblings, nieces and nephews, Maggie could not feel grounded until her three offspring arrived. Kelly landed that

Friday evening and the grim news became a confirmation of the premonition she had acted on.

"I wish I could have spoken with him one last time," Kelly lamented in her mother's arms, "but you know, I had a brilliant dream on the plane—he was running up a green slope, laughing gleefully and doing cartwheels. I think he was letting me know how wonderful he felt, how delighted he was."

"That does sound lovely," Maggie sniffled, thinking how much she would like to have his joyful laughter ringing in her ears rather than his frustrated, fearful shouts.

"That dream gave me a lot of peace," Kelly sighed, reaching for a tissue, "I don't even feel like myself."

Maggie kissed her forehead, "All things considered, you do seem quite serene," she said, putting her arm around Kelly's waist and guiding her toward the kitchen. She filled the kettle for tea, while Kelly laid out saucers and cups, and they sliced some bread and cheese, for the conversation would continue into the night.

Marie arrived the next day on the noon flight, and Lizzy by midnight. The available beds and rooms had been taken on a first-come first-served basis, so that when Lizzy got to the house, minus her suitcase, which had been left behind by the airline, she was directed to her late father's room where an air mattress had been set up.

For a few years, Maggie and Angelo had not been sharing a room because of his snoring, their differing schedules, and his aches and pains.

"It's eerie in here, without his bed," Lizzy said, clutching her purse and the tiny bathroom bag the airline had given her to make up for the missing luggage.

"I know," Kelly whispered, "we all felt weird about sleeping in here."

"And we thought, since you are the one with the see-through friends…" Marie chimed in, excusing the fact they had called dibs on the other rooms.

"We had to throw out the mattress," Maggie said, bringing home to the girls what the night he'd been taken away might have looked like. "It was custom sized anyway, so I had the frame removed too."

The four of them stood in the doorway, hesitating.

"Well," Lizzy said, breaking from the group and tossing her toiletry kit into the bathroom sink, bemoaning her absent luggage, "I'll need to borrow some pajamas, and something to wear tomorrow for the funeral."

"How infuriating this must be for you," Maggie sympathized, "but we'll find something in my closet that will do nicely—not to worry."

Kelly and Marie offered lotions, make up, deodorant, and anything else their sister might need.

Lizzy gave them a watery smile, remarking, "I guess the good news is, my grieving energy will be toned down tomorrow by the awkward feel of clothes that aren't mine and shoes half a size bigger."

Tilting her head toward the sound of slippers, padding briskly on floorboards, Marie said, "Here she comes."

"It's nearly two in the morning," Maggie admonished them, handing Lizzy a clean nightshirt, "and we have to be up early tomorrow."

As in years gone by, three voices replied, "Good night, mom," and followed it with a kiss and a tight hug.

"I'm so glad you are all here," Maggie sniffled.

Chapter
38

T he sliver of light under Maggie's bedroom door went out.

Kelly and Marie knocked softly on the door to their father's room and went in.

Lizzy sat on the air mattress, waiting for them.

"Well?" Kelly said in a quavering voice. She and Marie sat on either side of the mattress facing their sister.

"Much as mom feels guilty about it, she didn't really leave him alone in the hospital—a bunch of the see-through people stayed with him, even after the sedatives had worked through him."

Marie squeezed Lizzy's hand, blinking away the tears, "You'll have to tell her that tomorrow. It will soothe her for sure."

"I will."

"Did he know he wasn't alone? Do you think he's mad at mom?" Kelly asked.

Lizzy tilted her head as if trying for better reception. "Not at first, but I think near dawn he realized his brother and sisters were there, and he went with them."

Marie bit her lip, "It hasn't fully hit her that he's gone. I'm worried about mom."

"As well you should—but keep in mind, he hasn't been gone a full two days yet."

"I can tell already that she is reacting with her usual I'll-tackle-this-head-on attitude," Kelly said in a dark tone, "when I got here yesterday, she seemed to be in high gear—how she usually gets before a big social event—counting how many people are going to show to the service tomorrow, I mean, today, and how many of them will come home with us after, and how much food we should plan on."

Marie nodded, "Yes, it seems she only wants to deal with the immediate and not the long term."

"Which, again, seems normal to me, seeing as how this just happened."

"Maybe you're right," Marie sniffled, wiping tears away with the back of her hand.

Kelly got up and returned with tissues from the bathroom. "We need to think about how we are grieving too and try to appreciate that the loss of a father is completely different than the loss of a husband."

"There's something to that. My ex isn't dead, but it was a loss nevertheless," Lizzy said matter-of-factly, "it's been over two years and I'm still trying to figure out who I am after being someone's wife for over twenty years."

"We should focus on reassuring her that it's OK to take her time, and letting her know she has our support, no matter how long it takes."

"I second that," Kelly and Lizzy said, and Kelly added, "let's get some sleep, if we can."

Chapter 38

After the hugs, the sniffles, and the kisses, the door closed behind them and Lizzy turned off the lamp. Her head hit the pillow and with eyes closed, she began to say her mantras. The see-through people vied for positions in her upcoming dream state, but she ignored them and plowed on.

"...for all the blessings in my life. Thank you for the support and inspiration you grant me, today and always. To you, my ancestors, angels, and spirits, I entrust my dad..."

Lizzy's tears spilled onto the pillow and after a time, sleep took her.

The air mattress groaned under a slight pressure.

"Dad," Lizzy mumbled drowsily.

He whispered something she couldn't understand. The see-through people tugged at the drapes. Lizzy hadn't known the drapes hid an entire door. Dazzling sunlight poured through its glass panes. Lingering rays, like fireflies, lit up the corners of the bedroom and Angelo, with his arm around his brother's shoulder, walked out the door, deep in lively conversation.

"I love you, my Lizzy," whispered the winking fireflies, over and over, until their light dimmed to darkness.

"I love you too, dad."

A straggler firefly zoomed over Lizzy's bed, close to her face. She could see the point of light through her eyelids. She woke herself up trying to swat it away, realizing it was a ray of sunlight, peeking through the curtain—warm on her cheek.

Time to rise, we bury our father today.

Chapter
39

This is supposed to be a mass for the dead, Lizzy thought, trying to catch Kelly or Marie's eye.

"...If I say to someone wicked, 'Evil- doer, you are to die,' and you do not speak to warn the wicked person to renounce such ways, the wicked person will die for this guilt..." the ill-prepared priest droned on.

Outraged, Lizzy turned to her mother, but Maggie only closed her eyes as if to say, *let it lie*.

The chapel was silent, but for the stifled coughs of the congregation and the voice of the novice preacher, quoting the readings as part of a homily he hadn't prepared. "...If he does not listen, take one or two others along with you: whatever the misdemeanor, the evidence of two or three witnesses is required to sustain the charge..."

Lizzy stood up; hands balled into fists at her sides. Through gritted teeth, she cut him off, "That will be enough!"

On either side of her, Kelly and Marie shifted uncomfortably, but she didn't care.

234

He looked up from his notes, perplexed, and she hissed at him, "Please move along to the next portion of this funeral mass."

"Let us pray," the priest stammered, motioning for everyone to stand.

Lizzy continued to glare at him as he spluttered through the liturgy. She wouldn't have been surprised if her dad had sat up in his coffin to complain. He had never been much for religious rituals, and with every passing day, Lizzy felt more and more that his legacy to her was what he always claimed to have for himself; a personal connection with God, without a middle man, or church, or priest.

The thought caused the corners of her mouth to twitch upward, and she let levity smooth over her annoyance.

When the service was over, they went to place their hands over the coffin before it was shut to be transported. They gazed upon their father's face one last time.

Lizzy glanced at Kelly and they exchanged a quizzical frown—was she imagining it? A subtle smile seemed to play on his lips!

"Lights and shadows," Kelly whispered gazing up at the skylight and the cottony clouds drifting lazily above.

Lizzy shrugged, taking the palm of her hand off the glass that prevented her from touching her father's chest. She joined her sisters around their mother.

People left in clusters to find their cars and get to the cemetery. The four of them were the last to leave though, as Maggie continued to chat with those excusing themselves from attending the burial. Eventually they got to their car, knowing that the high traffic areas

and the time of day would not allow for a coordinated procession to follow the hearse.

Lizzy didn't speak, content to listen to her sisters and their mother discuss the best route to the location of the plot. It made her sad to see all the graffiti on the outside of the cemetery walls, thankfully, once inside, the grounds, and gravesites, were well-tended.

After a few turns and ups and downs, they spotted the crowd of family members who had already arrived at the site.

Heartfelt words were said. His favorite end-of-the-party song was sung, causing ripples of laughter among the mourners, in whose memories lingered decades worth of festive, carefree times. As the coffin was lowered into the ground and the singing faded, the smiles gave way to fresh tears.

Back at the house, they hastened to change into comfortable clothes. The dozen or so family members expected to join them, had begun to arrive. Multiple conversations ensued, in the kitchen, at the dining room table, in the sitting room. At any given time, they ate, laughed, cried, or held one another.

"Can you believe that priest!" Lizzy fumed, refusing to let go of her beef with the service, "doing a regular Sunday mass, even with the open casket right there!"

"That was awkward and inappropriate," Maggie conceded, "fortunately, he was more startled than affronted by your insolence."

"My insolence?" Lizzy bristled, although the risk she had taken of being chastised in public did make her squirm a little. "He had no right to be affronted when he was, like an idiot, preaching about evil doers and their wicked ways, and filling up a collection basket instead of, if nothing else, a simple prayer for the dead, Jesus!"

"Lizzy!" Maggie and Marie exclaimed in unison.

Kelly chimed in to de-escalate, "I think dad was watching and probably having a good laugh over it."

"That's for sure," Lizzy said under her breath.

Visitors didn't leave until late in the evening. One of the cousins took Lizzy to the airport to recover the suitcase, arriving in the midnight flight. When she got back home, her mother and sisters were still up, so it was two in the morning again before they went to bed.

Staring at the ceiling, after saying her mantras, Lizzy again tuned into the voices whispering in the dark, *changes coming, lots of changes.*

"No shit," she muttered and then, "amen to that."

Chapter
40

Monday dawned sunny and realistic.

Together, the four women tackled the list of practicalities that would legally transform them into the survivors of a husband and a father. Visits were made to insurance agencies, county clerks, the embassy, and banks. Wherever walk-ins were not welcome, they made appointments.

On a Wednesday afternoon, the call came from the hospital with the results from the battery of tests they had done when Angelo was admitted. The news that cancer had taken over his entire body and was the cause of death shocked everyone.

"What?" Lizzy let herself drop into a chair in the family room.

"And here we were, prepared for long years of gradually declining health—mental health!" Kelly said in a daze.

"Sweet Mary, mother of God! I should have dragged him to the hospital years ago," Maggie cried, a fresh wave of guilt washing over her.

"Mom, lymphoma is very aggressive," Marie observed, "and as much as he hated hospitals, there is no way he would've submitted to treatment."

"Of course, you're right," Maggie sniffed, "I guess this is exactly as he would have preferred it."

Through the whole week, they left promptly after breakfast and came back for lunch. Errands resumed in the afternoon, keeping them away until dinner in a bureaucratic frenzy that drove Lizzy up a wall.

Maggie retired to bed by ten that night, exhausted.

"I'm so glad we're here to help her with all this stuff," Marie called from the bathroom, with a toothbrush in her mouth.

Sitting lotus style on the bed, Lizzy rubbed moisturizer on her face. "Of course, you're right, and I need to complain less about all this stuff that needs to get done because it's not about me! I tell you though, I can totally see why dad used to get so upset. Remember when he went to renew his driver's license?"

Kelly laughed, "I talked with him that afternoon—I could hardly understand what he was saying—he was in such a rage, all grouchy and growling."

Teeth brushed; Marie came to sit by Lizzy, "Did you notice, mom didn't flat-out reject the notion of moving to California?"

Kelly joined in, clean-faced and in flannels, "With any luck, she might be acclimated to the idea before we head back home in another week."

"It won't be easy," Marie said, "there is a lifetime here that she'll need to deconstruct."

Lizzy recapped her moisturizer and frowned.

Remembering the prophetic voices in the night, she did an about face on her previous stance, "It might be just what she needs.

What if she's sort of excited about the opportunity for so much change?"

"Just a few days ago, you said it could take years for her to even come to terms with losing a husband."

"She can't have dealt with it already," Marie agreed.

"Although," Kelly mused, "I do see what you're saying, Lizzy, and maybe all it is, is that with dad having been sick for so long, she had already run that reel in her mind—you know—of what her life was going to look like without him. She is all about planning, as we well know."

Lizzy nodded but Marie shook her head. "I think the whole thing hasn't really hit her, and when it does, she will fall apart. She's already acting atypically, I mean, when have you known her to be OK to depend on others?"

"You have a point there."

"Maybe we're picking apart her every reaction because it distracts us from our own mourning," Kelly suggested turning the tables on the discussion.

"There's that too...."

The three sisters pondered in silence.

"Bottom line is we all grieve in different ways and in our own time," Kelly declared.

Marie jumped on board with that, "Agreed."

"For my part and for whatever reason, I can't bring myself to wail at the heavens over dad's death," Lizzy said, "instead, all I keep thinking about is how lucky my kids and I were to have spent a whole month here with him, not knowing we were going to lose him in two months."

Flashing her dimpled smile, Kelly intoned, "Ditto, it was like a cosmic blessing for me and my kids too."

Holding up her index finger, Marie clarified, "Divine intervention."

Lizzy grinned, "Or mom's planning. After all, she was anticipating the deterioration of his mind, and she wanted us to spend time with him before he was too far gone."

"You see what I mean?" Marie returned, "she was planning, doing her thing, right up until he died, and now..."

"Now she has to deal with the shock of him not lingering for years, like she had pictured he would."

Marie nodded, "We keep going in circles, and I guess that's how we're going to grieve too—in circles."

"Visiting and revisiting not only our feelings and reactions, but hers too."

"And we better be up to rehashing attitudes as changes spring up," Lizzy warned.

"She'll have a hard time with that," Marie predicted.

Chapter
41

"Rehashing attitudes as changes spring up."

Lizzy's words crackled in Maggie's ears as she walked back to her room—empty handed. She had gone to get the water pitcher she kept on her nightstand, but her intent was forgotten in eavesdropping on her daughters' conversation.

So much truth in their words, she fretted, quietly closing her door. *And here I thought I had been hiding my confusion like a proper mother and widow should.*

A widow... Maggie's mind tumbled back to Angelo's funeral.

Tucked in a corner of the chapel, the day of the service, a ghost from the past had appeared to her. His burning eyes bore into Maggie's until she blinked, and then Alonzo, like Angelo, was gone. The spectral quality of his appearance had completely removed her from the sober moment. So powerful was the vision that Maggie had not been able to think straight from then on, under constant attack from dusty memories and forgotten sensations.

Flustered by the recollection, as it went through her again, Maggie tried to figure out if the vision had been meant as a distraction—by

Lizzy's see-through people—to help her cope with grief. Or had she done it all on her own, to avoid reality with flights of fancy.

Like her girls said, she hadn't dismissed the idea of returning to California, even after thirty years. And that was part of her bewilderment, wasn't it? She hadn't wanted to leave in the first place, but when Angelo gave her no choice, she followed her husband. She made a home for him and created what became their livelihood.

Jardines LunaRosa, even now, was the magical place from which her daughters' lives had sprung.

The garden had financed their education and their travels. At LunaRosa they experienced what it meant to create and nurture something—to put one's essence into something and see what came of it. They had blossomed in the safety of the garden and had dreamed up their lives, eventually forming their own families.

In truth, Maggie and Angelo had already begun the long conversation of making a return to California, to be closer to their daughters and grandchildren.

"We must not be hasty," he had said, and she agreed. "At our age we have to foresee and avoid eventualities that could become impositions on our girls."

But for the past two years, Angelo's declining health stalled those plans. He could no longer participate in the daily operation of the garden, which was just as well, since Maggie had dependable, well-trained personnel. Her daily presence there was more out of habit than necessity, which left her with a great deal of time in her hands.

That's where her confusion started, even before Angelo died.

Maggie began to act and think of herself as a woman on her own, and that had predictable consequences.

The ease with which she slipped into widowhood, the uptick in energy, the prospect of selling her magnum opus, the reluctant excitement of setting up a new home, without consulting anyone's heart but her own, overpowered her grief to the point she wondered if she even felt it.

At that juncture, Maggie couldn't distinguish between guilt, practicality, or denial.

She pulled out a matchbook from the top dresser drawer and lit a candle. "Archangel Raphael, please watch over me as I sleep. Shine your light on me that I might see the way," Maggie crossed herself and got into bed.

Much as she loved her daughters, and although she would never say it to them, she wished they would return to their homes already. She knew their hearts were in the right place, but Maggie didn't need them treating her like an invalid or trying to analyze and decipher her every thought or move! What next? Would they take it upon themselves to make decisions for her?

"I'm plenty capable of sorting this out by myself, thank you very much!" she muttered, surrendering to a fitful slumber in the flickering candlelight.

The candle burned down to a stub while Maggie slept. Disoriented by the overcast morning, she did a double take on the clock, "Oh my! Eight-twenty!"

The girls were already in the kitchen, helping themselves to whatever they wanted for breakfast.

"If it isn't the sleeping beauty," Marie teased.

"I had a hard time falling asleep, but when I finally did, I was completely out!" Maggie yawned; the overheard conversation came back to her as she hugged and pecked each of her girls on the cheek.

She sat at the table that had already been set, feeling closely observed.

"I slept really good too," Kelly said, setting a bowl with papaya in front of Maggie, "it drizzled outside for a couple of hours, I could hear drops hit the window with the breeze, and it felt so good to be snuggled up in a warm bed."

"Everything looks sparkly clean outside," Maggie noted looking out of the window at the two fat birds bathing in the bowl. Angelo had set that up for them long ago.

She ate her fruit distractedly. Raphael wouldn't fail her—he must not—at some point that morning, she wanted to see the way forward.

"What's on the agenda today—are we almost done with errands?" Lizzy wondered, taking a sip of her coffee.

Marie, the calendar keeper, replied, "Only two official business appointments this afternoon. Mass this Sunday will be in dad's name, so we have to be there, and that's it until we go back home."

"I'm so thankful you are all here to help me with this process," Maggie surprised herself with the words coming out of her mouth. She had meant to affirm the stability of her faculties, not play into their fanciful conjectures of denialism and vulnerability.

She waved off their choruses of 'you're welcome' and 'of course.'

"All the legalities of the case are just too much for me to have handled alone, and I can trust none but you three with all of it."

"Do you want us to stay longer, maybe?" Kelly offered, looking from Lizzy to Marie, but Maggie shook her head.

"I know you two need to get back to work, and Kelly, since you're the one with the most flexibility, it would be so much better if you came again in a couple of months for a follow up," Maggie smiled, squeezing Kelly's hand and catching the fleeting glances between the three girls.

"I don't want to make rash decisions, but with your father gone, I am contemplating a move back to California more seriously."

A wave of relief seemed to wash over the girls as they called out their replies, oldest to youngest.

"Of course!"

"No rash decisions!"

"For sure! Let's talk it over in the coming months and see how best to manage it."

And that was the beginning of the year long conversation to come, complete with rehashing of attitudes and unexpected changes.

Chapter
42

As the weeks went by, the uprooting Maggie had offered to contemplate became a certainty.

In the five months, between the middle of September, when the girls returned to their homes, and Maggie's birthday in February, it had been settled between them that they would return for the one year anniversary of their father's death, and to say farewell to an era of their lives.

Maggie, with the barest of essential belongings, would return to California with her daughters to start from scratch.

March was spent in a flurry of plotting how best to dismantle the life she had built. A candle burned on her dresser, from sunup until sundown, beneath a card with the likeness of Archangel Raphael, worn from years of fervent prayer.

Maggie's life's work must bear bountiful fruit so that her retirement living wouldn't require her to make sacrifices or impose on her family.

From her client roster, she handpicked promising buyers for Jardines LunaRosa. Of course, she would resort to that list only after speaking

with the garden's site managers, they had been with her from the beginning and deserved first option.

April blew in, giving Maggie a sense of buoyancy as she began to execute her well-laid strategy.

"I told you the meeting would go well if you waited until the full moon!" Kelly gushed on their conference call Friday evening.

"And you didn't forget to fill a crystal bowl with water, and set it on top of slips of paper with all the participants names on them, right?"

"No, Miss Lizzy, I didn't forget."

"Ok, ok, but how did you guys leave it? What did the managers say?" Marie pressed.

"They were surprised and dismayed to hear that I am leaving. But, of course, they were grateful for the ample notice and their options. They want to meet among themselves to see about making an offer. They've asked for a week to think about it."

"Sounds reasonable," and "Yes, it does," came the satisfied replies.

"Wait, someone is calling on my cell phone," Maggie put down the handset and answered the unknown caller. "Hello."

A male voice came through the phone line, "How is Maggie, the magnificent, faring these days?"

The color rose to her cheeks at the impudent greeting, "Who is this?"

"It's my curse to be forgettable."

Chapter 42

The self-deprecating jest irritated Maggie, more so because, although familiar, she could not place the voice. Flustered and aware that the girls were listening, she stammered, "I am on the other line."

He started to say something, maybe offer to call back at a better time, but she flipped the phone shut as if it had spewed fire into her ear.

"Where were we," she said into the handset, her voice sounding shrill to her own ears.

"Who was that?" Lizzy asked.

"Oh, just one of those telemarketers," Maggie lied, hand on her chest trying to calm her beating heart, grateful that the girls were not there to see the furious blush burning her cheeks.

The identity of the caller at last came to her; one of her distributors, one she hadn't done business with in over two years. Manuel Herrera.

"So, they'll let you know a week from now if they have an offer—I'm sure it will be a good one," Kelly rejoined.

"Yes, yes—I think it will be. But listen, girls, it's getting late over here, and it's been a long day."

"Of course! Goodnight, mom, and congratulations!" Marie cheered.

Kelly and Lizzy expressed similar sentiments and wished her a goodnight.

"And a goodnight to you, my darling daughters," she sang, and with a final "God bless you," Maggie put the handset slowly back in its cradle.

She stared at the cell phone still clutched in her other hand, bewildered by the unexpected development. Thoughts and sensations,

like flashes, competed for recognition, but she continued to stare blankly, as if at a lightning storm in a distant horizon.

I wonder if he'll call back.

Do I want him to call back?

Out of patience with herself—cheeks still flushed—Maggie groaned, "I'm not a high-school girl."

Yet the level of angst she was experiencing could only be compared to what she felt, all those years ago, as she prepared to meet with Alonzo at the theater.

Unbidden, the memory of the forgotten bundle of letters she locked away pierced her mind. Maggie's heart threatened to beat right out of her chest. Both Angelo and Alonzo were dead. Had Alonzo appeared to her to blame her for their unrealized love? And when had she last drawn breath?

She inhaled, and with the oxygen came a head rush. Falling back onto her pillows, Maggie flipped the phone open and stared at the number displayed.

I could call him back.

She rolled over onto her stomach stifling an even louder groan. *Where did these distractions and memories come from?*

Maggie's path forward, in California with her daughters and grandchildren, could not be clearer; Mary, the angels and the stars had all conspired to make it so. She would not give in to temptation.

Calling that number would be to defy divine providence—was there any other way of looking at it?

Chapter
43

Under the influence of the full moon, the vexing phone call and the swift passage of forty-eight hours, couldn't help but trigger a profound alteration in Maggie's mind. So it was that when Manuel called back, not only did Maggie take the call, but she heard herself dishing out flirty comebacks to the flurry of praises he heaped upon her.

For the first time in decades, Maggie gave in. She chose to see herself through someone else's eyes, relinquishing a substantial measure of the self-control that had shaped her, and served her so well in the past.

"You are a sought-after commodity," Manuel assured her, "a successful, good-looking woman in the prime of her life."

Besides resonating with Maggie's secret view of herself, his words offered her new vistas. With a mystified grin, drunk on the belief that she was indeed, in the prime of her life, Maggie took in a revelation, *only my antiquated beliefs prevent me from tackling second chances.*
The earth rotated some more. And when the waxing moon looked in on Maggie, it was to complete the alchemy by infusing her

day-to-day with a fresh silvery vibe, which she projected to captivating effect.

Two more suitors drifted into her orbit. The levity with which she handled the budding relationships spurred on a sense of youthful invincibility, along with the intense conviction that her time was at hand, to do as she pleased, for herself.

Maggie spoke to her girls, separately, a few times per week. She liked it that way, the better to fend off their bemused inquiries. Maggie wasn't ready to confess what had been going on in their absence.

That the girls puzzled over the levels of buoyancy their mother had never been known for, only increased the hilarity at Maggie's end.

Mother's Day came and as planned; Kelly, Lizzy and Marie, who were together to celebrate the holiday, initiated the scheduled conference call that Sunday morning.

"So—" Kelly segued after the hoopla of 'Happy Mother's Day' wishes died down, "we conducted a remote intervention last Monday with the full moon."

A tense silence took the air out of the phone line until a terse, "And?" blew in from south of the border.

"We tried to reach you, but you were obscured."

"Almost like you were hiding from us behind a silver veil."

Through starts and stops, so as not to talk over one another, Kelly, Lizzy and Marie continued on that vein, aimed at getting a reply from Maggie as to what had come over her.

Maggie shuddered at the sudden vision of them, not as the women they were at present, but as elementary school girls, sitting in a circle. Maggie saw a photo of herself in their midst, surrounded by candles—all Kelly's doing—Maggie knew.

And the little girls had seen her, from three thousand miles away! 'Behind a silver veil' Lizzy had said.

"From our phone calls, I thought we were dealing with isolated occurrences," Kelly went on, "but we've compared notes, and now we think something has happened. Something has changed you from the temperate and traditional person we know, to, to—"

"To what?" Maggie snapped, feeling trapped in their candlelit circle.

"Mom, are you regressing?" Lizzy blurted.

Maggie let out a silvery laugh, relieved to confirm that their information was incomplete, but that initial reaction was soon tempered. She understood that her daughters had taken a change on her part, even one that made her feel good, as evidence that she was malfunctioning!

Maggie recovered and rejoined, somewhat defensively, with, "Your father died eight months ago, I'm dismantling my entire life! I'm going through a mixture of grief for our loss, and satisfaction for a job well done. I'm also reconnecting with business acquaintances to smooth the garden's path forward," she threw in the last in a sly, careless tone. Somewhere down the road she would need to introduce the subject of a suitor—as soon as she settled on one them.

Maggie didn't need to be face-to-face with her girls to see the shifty glances they exchanged on hearing her pronouncement. Marie's next words confirmed it.

"We worry you might be dealing with too much, mom, how I wish we could be there sooner to help you with everything."

"I can handle things just fine!" Maggie assured them, fearful of losing the four months she still had to herself. She dismissed them with, "Your plan to come over at the end of August is perfect! That's when things will get really hairy, what with emptying the house, packing and whatnot."

They said their goodbyes and, overall, Maggie felt she had mollified their immediate concerns. Just in case though, she would watch her tone going forward and would try not to share as much.

Alas, far from keeping things under wraps, Maggie became more spirited and daring than ever, incited by the influence of her male callers.

The lucrative sale of Jardines LunaRosa to the managers elevated her confidence to cosmic levels—the world was her oyster—financial independence, romance, health, why, Maggie needn't do anything she didn't want to!

The weeks evaporated, and in that time, her pesky girls increased their phone calls in tag-team fashion. To her dismay, they read through every toned-down effusion about outings or gatherings, forcing Maggie to discourage the two later arrivals in favor of just Manuel.

Even with that concession, much to Maggie's irritation, Kelly, surely in cahoots with the other two, declared a happy change of plans. She was flying in—a whole month in advance—to help sort out the liquidation of household items and kick off the packing efforts.

Affronted by her daughters' obvious lack of faith in her abilities, Maggie simpered, "Of course, my darling girl, thank you so much for your thoughtfulness!"

In two weeks' time, Maggie would no longer have the run of her house.

Sulking, she called Manuel. Her ill humor simmered down when the phone rang, but he didn't answer.

"Drat!" She flipped the phone shut without leaving a message.

Rethinking it, she started to redial, but the memory of harsh admonitions directed at the girls, struck her, like a physical slap.

I'm not raising flirts, no daughter of mine will ever chase after a man!

After months of flying high, the single recollection put Maggie squarely in her daughters' minds, for it spoke volumes about how they looked at her.

Confusion set in.

All her life, Maggie had believed in leading by example and with integrity, and within that frame, a change of heart had to be preferable to a double standard.

I should have been more open with my girls instead of making them spy on me through silly candle flights.

"I can't very well take it back," she muttered, "they'll all be here soon enough anyway."

Manuel returned the missed call, just as she had climbed into bed. Maggie told him straightaway of Kelly's impending arrival. Not feeling up to a long conversation, she made her excuses and they hung up wishing each other sweet dreams.

Maggie turned out the light and started to say her prayers but kept getting sidetracked by nagging thoughts—*hypocrisy or change of heart.*

Whatever the case, her recent ruminations were to blame for dulling the sheen of her romantic conversations with Manuel. So immersed was Maggie in how he made her feel and think, that she could not see the storm brewing.

When Kelly arrived, Maggie thought it would be appropriate to first introduce him, in the best light, of course, and then gradually ease her daughter into the role Manuel played in her life. But she underestimated Kelly, ever the radar, who picked up on every emotion emitted around her.

Maggie thought she was gently introducing Manuel, yet what Kelly saw and reported to her sisters, as Maggie would later find out, were a slew of alarming changes she was seeing with her own eyes. Had she heard Kelly's urgent whispers on the phone, she would have been mortified.

"When the phone rings—believe it or not—our seventy-six-year-old mother changes color, like a schoolgirl. Remember Lizzy how you always used to blush for no reason at all? Well, she runs to her room and closes the door. And get this, she goes out for hot chocolate, she listens to songs he plays to her over the phone! The only redeeming something in this fresh devilry, is that at least it's down to a single gentleman caller, *Manuel*, is his name. Can you believe it, just a few weeks ago there used to be two other hopefuls!"

Since Kelly didn't confront her, Maggie relaxed.

Together, they attended to practicalities, chattering away and making plans, careful to avoid an open discussion of the frequent calls, or the caller for that matter. The days passed so pleasantly that Maggie began to look forward to the arrival of Lizzy and Marie, nurturing a bubble of hope that they would understand her flourishing aspirations.

Kelly continued to neither reproach nor celebrate anything having to do with Manuel. Although Maggie would have preferred a warmer acknowledgement of her choice of him in her life, she was satisfied that there hadn't been a flat-out rebuke.

Encouraged, Maggie went on anticipating Lizzy and Marie's arrival, aware of an unusual sense of sisterhood coloring her hopes. She wondered where the maternal joy of gathering her children around her had gone, and handily concluded that the last twenty-five years had transformed her girls into wives and mothers themselves.

If she granted them an equal state of womanhood, wouldn't that go a long way to justify the behavior disparities the girls worried about?

Of course!

It did not occur to Maggie that her girls might not be ready to see their mother as an equal.

If she suspected it, it was at a subconscious level; one moment, Maggie was persuaded that their vibrations were aligned, the next, it was as if she missed a step on a staircase. On the night she and Kelly went to the airport, a skittish Maggie, pale and silent, sat in the passenger seat, convinced she had misjudged everything.

Why, at that very moment, Lizzy and Marie were barreling toward home, riding the fearsome Trade winds, like witches on jetted broomsticks. They would join Kelly within the hour and put her, their own mother, on trial for her inconsistencies!

At a loss, Maggie began tra-la-la-ing along with the radio, hoping to subdue her misgivings. It didn't help that out of the corner of her eye, she thought she saw Kelly grin.

Chapter 44

M aggie needn't have worried that night, for her girls had decided in advance they would not broach the subject of Manuel until the evening after their arrival.

The pleasant day spent with her girls had the unfortunate effect of ratifying to Maggie their impending approval. So, when Manuel's daily phone call came, she blithely disappeared into her room, conscious of giving them an opportunity to discuss the subject among themselves.

Over dinner, meaning to rouse their sympathy, Maggie alluded to the crux of her change of heart; the conundrum she had been trying to solve for months.

"When I went to New York in the sixties, I meant to put down roots there," she began, pausing on each expectant face, the better to hold their attention, "but your father brought us back here, and although I didn't like it at first, divine providence revealed this to be the new grounds from where we would flourish. When your *abuelita* Dolores, God rest her soul, sent my rose cuttings, I knew this would be their new home, and ours."

The girls nodded.

Heartened, Maggie continued, "And what a life and home we've had here! That is why, through the efforts to dismantle it all, I've come to wonder...Are we doing the right thing?"

The nodding ceased, giving way to suspicious glances.

Just that afternoon, Manuel had asked if she was sure about what she meant to do, and now, she had actually repeated that statement to her daughters! What would they think of her, if they knew Maggie, their mother, had allowed someone to put words in her mouth?

She shifted gears. Dancing around his influence over her, she put the focus on common ties between her and the girls.

"We'll be leaving behind more than half of the family, and what of all the loyal friends we have here?"

The plaintive sentence hung in the air, unchallenged, for the space of a heartbeat. Kelly drew in her breath; Marie raised her eyebrows; and Lizzy frowned.

"The other half of the family is in the United States," Marie rejoined.

"As social as you are, and with the inviting energy you put out, there is no doubt you will have an extensive new circle of friends in no time," Kelly asserted.

As if to bypass the trivial and get to the heart of the matter, Lizzy opted for a shrewd parable.

"Mom, when people found out I was divorced, a lot of men called on me—family friends, even married men! Confessing to being attracted to me, assuring me they would value me in ways my ex-husband would never be able to. Spotlighting the characteristics they thought

I wanted to hear about before making their proposals; beautiful, intelligent, at *the prime of my life*. 'Won't you let me show you the world? First-class all the way. My wife won't ever know.'"

Blindsided by Lizzy's blunt delivery of such a parallel, Maggie could only stare at her. She wouldn't even look at the other two but could tell their glances shifted nervously toward her.

It hit Maggie, out of nowhere, that her daughters knew exactly what she had been up to. They knew where her doubts originated, and they knew what she was contemplating. Their measured response and coordinated stance, both impressed and irritated her.

"There was no trusting any of those men, Mom," Lizzy went on, "they were looking to please only themselves and didn't care who they took advantage of to get what they wanted."

That did it, *Manuel is no opportunist!*

"If you don't mind, I am a fairly decent judge of character," Maggie cautioned, dropping all pretenses, "I can see you, all of you, have made assumptions that have nothing to do with reality."

"We have been respecting your silence, giving you the space to share at your convenience," Kelly said, putting her hand over Maggie's.

"All we could do was make assumptions because your words led in one direction, but your actions seemed to take you in another," Marie pleaded.

Part of Maggie wanted to come clean and own that she shouldn't have kept her daughters in the dark, but it was too late for that.

"I can understand why this would be hard for someone like you," Lizzy observed, and Maggie bristled.

"What do you mean, someone like me?"

"Up until now you have been traditional to a fault, throughout our upbringing, your business dealings, with your family and social network. How can we not make assumptions, when Dad hasn't been dead a year yet, and you're letting an impeccable track record of honor and fidelity come into question."

"What?"

"If you are hiding Manuel from extended family and your general acquaintance, which you are, it's because you know they will consider it a hasty, highly suspect development," Kelly said in her best, soothing tone.

"And, Mom, you probably feel that way yourself, don't you? That it is hasty?" Marie implored.

"Do you all feel this way?" Maggie demanded, feeling betrayed and willfully ignoring the part of her that agreed with her daughters.

Kelly and Marie replied with a contrite nod.

Not Lizzy, a lighthearted grin played on her lips, "Mom, if it's dating you want, there will be plenty of opportunity in California."

The cheeky comment riled Maggie, not only because she thought it brazen, but because it implied Lizzy didn't like her choice of a date.

"I am seventy-five-years old, and I believe I have earned my right to do as I please, without consulting anyone."

"We understand and agree. But are you willing to give up on your expectations of those whom you won't be consulting? Us, for example," Kelly reasoned, still in her most holistic-doctoral tone.

"I, for one, would be perfectly happy not to return here, ever," Lizzy declared, "you can see what drama that would be, if you chose to stay."

Tears glittered in Marie's brown eyes, but they didn't spill. "Let's say you do as you please. You stay here and make a life with a man we don't know. You will expect us to visit you, to spend time here and incorporate ourselves to a reality you have chosen, won't you?"

"That's an expectation we likely won't meet, because we would no longer be coming to our home—it would be yours and his," Kelly asserted, but immediately shifted the negative intensity of the argument to a more positive probability, "you have always been, and will continue to be, a woman of means, so there is no reason why you couldn't come see us and your grandchildren, as often as your new obligations allow it."

Maggie's eyes narrowed. Her next words slashed through the air, "So, my own daughters begrudge me a second chance at happiness."

Lizzy winced. Kelly and Marie shook their heads vehemently.

"Mom, through our teenage years, if a boy asked for a date, your biggest fear was that we would allow that boy undue influence. 'Keep your head about you, know yourself, mind your plans and your family. Don't discard permanence for the novel excitement of an unknown factor', that's what you drilled into our heads for years."

"That is all true, Marie, but I'm not a teenager. I am your mother," Maggie protested, inwardly repeating to herself that it was a change of heart, it had never been a double standard.

"Well, you have certainly been acting like an adolescent this whole month," Kelly smirked, but Maggie erased the traces of amusement with a well-aimed, fierce glance at her eldest.

Lizzy put up her hand, requesting to intervene, "The bottom-line question is, will you change plans that have been a year in the making, over three months' worth of sweet talk?"

Maggie pursed her lips, enraged over how her own words had been used against her. But from then on, all talk of staying ceased.

Chapter
46

F eeling that she had once again given in to her girls, Maggie let them engage in make-up favors to herself—it was the least they could do after putting her on trial.

To acknowledge their mother's concession, the girls spoiled her rotten.

Maggie set tasks for them and they scurried to comply. They cheerfully planned meals, which Kelly and Marie prepared. Lizzy, who had missed out on the cooking gene, could only be counted on for clean-up duty. They attended family gatherings and going-away engagements. They scheduled utility shut offs, they packed and cleaned tirelessly, until the house was ready to be turned over to new owners.

"Mom, what should I do with—" Lizzy called from somewhere upstairs one afternoon.

Maggie came up, followed by Kelly and Marie. They found Lizzy sitting lotus style on the floor with an old hat box. An assortment of letters, photographs, and postcards were strewn about her.

"It was tucked in the top shelf of your closet," Lizzy said, holding up two ancient airmail envelopes, "can we?"

Maggie bit her lip on recognizing Alonzo's letters—the two she had not burned. She nodded, murmuring, "It's been over fifty years."

Tapping the postmark on one of the envelopes and with an arch smile, Lizzy said, "You got these before you were married."

"Very observant."

Maggie sat on her mattress on the floor, the bed frames were long gone, and together, they pored over Alonzo's letters; the one preceding his trip to New York City, and the one he sent from Lima.

"… Rest assured that the merest hint of a change of heart from you will have me on the next flight out, and at your doorstep! Yours forever and always, Alonzo." Kelly finished reading, eyes twinkling over the ill-fated romance.

Lizzy praised his writing style, but Marie's troubled expression hinted at her rejection of any shadow on the history of her parentage.

"What's all this about, Mom?"

Maggie related the thwarted love story that led to her marrying their dad. While caught up in the memories, she smiled fondly at her daughters' rapt expressions.

"It was written in the stars that Angelo had to be your father," she mused, struck by the notion that without him, these three women, as they were, would not exist.

With a wistful sigh, she closed that chapter of her life with, "I only saw Alonzo twice after we said goodbye that rainy day in New York.

Once at a party, where we didn't speak at all. And then, I saw his ghost at your dad's funeral. The fact is, I knew very little of him, I don't even know when he died."

Lizzy went to bed that night, her head full of Alonzo's story and the novel idea that the stars mapped out her and her sisters' entry into the world. Fancy that—it had been written in the cosmos that they would be born only to Maggie and Angelo!

They were getting on a plane in seventy-two hours, never to return, and the thought of it had Lizzy in a distracted state. Even when it came to her nightly mantras; no sooner did she invoke ancestors and faeries, that her mind wandered.

She dozed without realizing it.

A wondrous sense of joy enveloped Lizzy as she feasted on the sight of *abuelita* Dolores. She knew right away it was a lucid dream, why, *abuelita* couldn't be more than thirty-five! Plump cheeks, eyes crinkling with laughter—feel of her rough fingertips on Lizzy's face.

A distant pang of realization threatened to wake her on the awkward air mattress. "Don't think it," she told herself, and focused harder on Dolores, who had rolled up her skirt and had already sat on the hot sand. With a lazy backstroke motion, *abuelita* had begun piling sand over her bare legs.

Smiling at the sweet familiarity of the moment—how many summers had they spent at the beach—Lizzy knelt beside her and began heaping mounds of warm, sugary sand on her feet while Dolores spoke.

"The Gemini constellation paused in the heavens the afternoon Maggie was conceived. There were cataclysmic forces at play."

Lizzy worked in unison with her grandmother, getting Dolores' legs good and covered; the hot sand easing the pain in her joints. *But* abuelita *couldn't possibly be suffering from arthritis, not at thirty-five and…* Lizzy waved away the doubts, "Must not wake up. Must not interrupt."

To the rhythmic roar of the waves, Dolores went on with the beautiful tale, and although she'd never heard it before, Lizzy knew it was true.

"The stars resumed their cosmic dance and swirled aloft for forty weeks, until Pisces swam in during the rainy season to flush Maggie right out of my womb. The ageless stars whispered about there being two twin souls for her. Had my Maggie understood their place in the cosmic timeline, she would have had an easier time. As it was, all she could do was embrace one and cast-off the other, as a threat to the moral life she intended to live. She locked the idea of him in a chest she refuses to open."

The wings of a seagull obliterated the sun, its cries mingled with the thundering waves. Lizzy swatted at the obstinate bird.

"Where is the chest?" she asked her grandmother.

Cawing, the seagull landed on the mound of sand. Dolores wiggled her toes and laughed.

The cries of the bird gradually became the artificial ringing of a phone, and Lizzy's eyes snapped open.

The dismal light coming through the curtains told her it couldn't be more than six in the morning. The tomblike hush of the empty home told Lizzy that the motherhouse of the merry-god-witches was no more.

Time to rise, it's the end of an era today.

Sunday morning.

The house was clean and nearly empty. All of Maggie's belongings had been packed into eight large suitcases—they had been weighed, packed again, and reweighed several times to ensure they were within airline requirements.

Nestled in one of the suitcases, in black bags lined with wet cotton, traveled the contraband rose cuttings and daisy starts.

By the front door stood four carry-on bags, jammed packed with essentials and whatever hadn't fit into the rest of their luggage.

"C'mon, c'mon! We're late for the anniversary mass already," Marie shooed everyone out the door. "We'll be back for this stuff after, on our way to the hotel."

Dogged by her dream of the night before and by her mother's words about her own daughters begrudging her a second chance at happiness, Lizzy shifted distractedly on the pew. She caught only snippets of the homily but was relieved to hear that, although it was a proper requiem, the predominant sentiment was that of celebrating her father's life.

Thinking that this service made up for the fouled-up one a year ago, Lizzy continued to brood until mass was over. Then, with the pastor's blessing, they were released into the sunlit courtyard, where

they graciously accepted everyone's condolences and well-wishes for their upcoming adventure.

"I can't help feeling that everything we're doing; we're doing for the last time," Lizzy remarked while they waited for a cab.

"Because we are," Maggie murmured somberly as the four them climbed into the vehicle.

After lunch at a local restaurant, they returned home for a last goodbye and a last walk-through Jardines LunaRosa.

On spotting the row of half-full birdfeeders, lightning flashed in Maggie's heart for a moment; the pang of lost innocence and the blessing of a flight, intermingled. Her grown girls walking beside her now, in the garden they helped build, were the beautiful embodiments of the real growth she had cultivated. And, like a bolt of lightning, the pain passed, though she would not hear the rumble of thunder or feel the reviving rain just yet.

Standing by the fountain in the greenhouse, looking about as if she didn't recognize the place, Kelly said, "Is it just me, or does this feel weird?"

Lizzy agreed, "It feels like it's not ours anymore."

"Because it isn't," Marie pointed out the obvious.

"It's strange that a signature on a paper can alter a whole lifetime," Maggie sighed, "but such is life, and a new era is beginning."

They collected their luggage and had to take two cabs to their hotel, near the airport, where they had reserved two adjacent rooms.

The girls left Maggie alone for her nap, and to let her say her goodbyes to Manuel.

Next door, sitting lotus style on the bed, Lizzy shared her distress in urgent whispers, "What she said last night made me feel so selfish—I think I really am begrudging her her happiness."

"I feel a little slighted, on behalf of our father," Marie admitted in an undertone.

Lizzy nodded, "I loved our father too, and I know what you mean— it's like she's moving on too soon. Then again, what is too soon? I just don't see Mom turning into the widow, dressed in black, until the day she joins him in the grave—she still has a lot of life in her."

Kelly sighed, "For my part, I think this guy is not the right one. Maybe because we haven't really met him, or because it's too soon for her to involve herself. For whatever reason, he just doesn't feel right. Or, *she* doesn't feel right to me, under his influence."

"You nailed it!" Lizzy aimed a finger gun at Kelly, "so if he's not the right influence, what if, for the heck of it, we tracked Alonzo down? You know, to find out when he died. Maybe he has kids and they know more about the missing letters. We can share his two letters and maybe they'll let us see the ones mom wrote to him, if he kept them."

"I don't know about that," Marie fretted, looking from Lizzy to Kelly.

"Oh, c'mon, what can it hurt—we won't tell Mom about it, unless we uncover something new."

While Lizzy appeased Marie, Kelly began searching on her phone.

"Oh my!"

Lizzy and Marie cried out, "What?"

Clustered around Kelly's cell phone, they found out that Alonzo was not dead. And judging from a social profile, he was a widower who, like Maggie, had children and grandchildren of his own.

"Click right there—right there," Lizzy urged, "let's get his email address!"

"We're leaving tomorrow—let's not be hasty—let's think on it," Marie cautioned.

"Who's thinking of doing anything today," Lizzy said, eyes glinting.

"Agreed," smiled Kelly, "we won't breathe a word about it to her, not even to correct her assumption that he is dead."

"Really, because what if he's not interested in her, maybe he has a girlfriend already," Marie said, with a hint of humor in her voice, at last, "you know how rampant love affairs are among seniors."

Their silvery laughter pierced the dusky atmosphere and the night's first star twinkled merrily at them.

Amid the hilarity and the decision that wine would flow on their last evening there, Lizzy's dream from the night before came back to her full force. She recounted it to Kelly and Marie, carefully paraphrasing *abuelita*'s words.

"Cosmic timing…" Kelly echoed dreamily.

"Wait, two twin souls for her? If one of them was dad, which of the other two is it?" Marie fussed, "what if Manuel is the second twin soul? What if we're taking her away from him?"

Lizzy shook her head, "I'm with Kelly on this one. Manuel is not it!"

Chapter
47

Through the entire return journey, minus the three-hour distraction of a connecting flight, the girls agonized about Lizzy's dream, and about judging their mother's choices.

Was it right to have made her choose between themselves and a partner she viewed as her second chance at happiness?

From their row across the aisle, the girls watched their mother.

With her neck support pillow firmly in place, Maggie slept.

Kelly whispered, "What if the stars are intervening, through us, to present her with a second chance at cosmically ordained bliss?"

Lizzy joined in the speculation, "Because Manuel isn't the one she locked up in a chest—Alonzo is. The stars and *abuelita* have given us a key to spring him out of there."

Marie kept her thoughts to herself.

It didn't take much to get Maggie settled in her new place. The fact that she had downsized from five to two bedrooms couldn't help but speed up the process.

The proximity of Maggie's sisters, for they would now be living within ten minutes from each other, made it so there were more hands on deck than needed, at all times. Everything from cleaning to potting rose cuttings and daisy starts, from furnishing to decorating, was accomplished in riotous waves of laughter, clashing opinions, and improvised outings.

Within a few weeks, Maggie's new motherhouse was in order, thoroughly infused with the energies of her daughters, grandchildren, and the merry-god-witches.

As the whirlwind of activity tapered off, Maggie began taking stock of her situation, and on a leisurely evening, with just Olivia visiting her, she at last let the thunder roll.

"Something occurred to me the other day," Maggie began, her glance drifting thoughtfully over the host of angel cards taped to the dresser mirror, the lit pillar reflected on it, and the Holy Face above her bedroom door, "I've spent too much time worrying about my girls not living the lives I imagined for them."

"That's what mothers do," Olivia soothed.

"I used to tell myself that children are borrowed treasures, that I need to let them be who they are, but I never really put that into practice."

"What do you mean? Your girls are doing great!"

"That's what I'm coming to realize. Angelo did hint at it once, but I ignored him. The truth is, unlike Marie, Kelly and Lizzy chose paths that didn't agree with what I had envisioned. I set out to steer them back on track, creating a great deal of stress for myself and heartache for them! I see now that I've stifled Kelly and Lizzy, long enough."

"You've always been bossy," Olivia smirked, seeming to allude to their high school years, "I can understand how irksome it is to you for two of your kids to deviate from your plan."

"Kelly with her holistic medicine, and Lizzy with her writing, it's like they're antagonizing me on purpose!" Maggie fumed.

"But they're not."

"Kelly said to me the other day that I had dreamed up LunaRosa and demanded that everyone believe in it like I did. She said I made them put their best energy into it because I knew its success depended on it. She asked, why was it OK for everyone to conspire with me to make my dream happen, yet from my heart, I would not do the same for my own daughters' dreams."

"And she's right—I mean—Maggie, it was pretty harsh to tell Lizzy that success comes to a writer only when they're dead."

"Oh! Do not repeat what I said! I feel awful about it—how stubborn I've been with the it's-my-way-or-the-highway attitude! How did I miss it for so long? They are doing exactly what I taught them to do; work hard, put their heart and their best effort into what they love!"

"So, what will you do about it?"

"The only thing I know how," Maggie said, finally letting the rain fall, "when is the new moon?"

By Halloween, barely forty-five days since Maggie had been transplanted, her team of bustling archangels, along with her attitude shift and her change of heart started to bear supernatural fruit. What wonders a little bit of rain can bring!

Patients seeking holistic healing came out of the woodwork to be seen by Kelly, and Lizzy's advertising campaigns, as if released from algorithm jail, began to pay for themselves with steady book sales.

Remarking on the cosmic shift in their fortunes, not knowing to what it was owed, but with Maggie's wistful countenance in mind—from when she told them about Alonzo—the girls revisited their plan to interview him.

As Thanksgiving neared, they began planning the feast; Maggie's first big holiday as a new resident of the state.

On November eleventh, they gathered at Marie's house.

"Since Thanksgiving is at your house this year, we may as well make all the preparations here too," Lizzy said, filling a crystal bowl with water and placing it on the kitchen counter, beneath the window. "There—it should get plenty of sun and moonlight in this spot."

Kelly lit three candles and set them on the dining room table, "Today's new moon bodes well for the new beginning—we'll ask our ancestors to guide us too."

Marie came in, looking over her glasses in teacherly fashion as she set down her laptop. "We're borrowing mom's angels too; you know how they do whatever she says. So, Raphael, you are hereby summoned."

Lizzy finished cutting the four slips of paper in which she had written their names and Alonzo's. She placed them under the bowl. To Marie, she said, "Remember to change the water every day."

They sat around the dining room table, pondering the content of an introductory email, and soon, Marie was clicking away on the keys, while Kelly and Lizzy made revisions on the go.

Satisfied with the finished product, they ended it with a request.

"If you are willing," Lizzy dictated, "we would like it if you joined us on a video call."

"This coming November the twenty-fifth," Kelly interjected. "It's perfect cause that's when the full moon is."

Kelly and Lizzy rose from their seats and peered over Marie's shoulder. They scanned the message on the screen one last time and hit the 'send' key.

They only had to wait two days. Alonzo's reply came in the affirmative, and it was all they could do not to move up the date of the conference call. But Kelly prevailed.

"Absolutely not! This call has to happen during the full moon."

Lizzy laughed, "You're right, that way he won't know what hit him."

Thank goodness for Maggie's obligatory nap in the afternoon. The girls hadn't considered that the full moon was the day before Thanksgiving!

Maggie was already at Marie's for the holiday weekend, so as an extra precaution, they took the laptop to her room upstairs. Behind closed doors, they initiated the video conference.

"He has to be as nervous as we are," Lizzy said in an undertone, just as the ringing ceased and the screen displayed 'connecting'.

They held their breath.

The man who appeared on the monitor had an iconic look about him. As one, the three girls sat up straighter and smiled.

"I can't express how delighted I am that Maggie's daughters have contacted me."

The husky voice suited Alonzo's more salt-than-pepper hair, and his unassuming features put them at ease right away.

"We are so pleased you agreed to it."

The effortless conversation lasted forty minutes, in which they heard his side of the story and they updated him on Maggie's. He confirmed to them that he had showed up at the funeral, but had thought it inappropriate to approach after all, so he had left without talking to her.

When the girls revealed their plan, he agreed at once to be Maggie's seventy-seventh birthday surprise.

"I understand the risk," he assured them, "if she is not pleased to see me, I will leave without complaint.

They closed the call with promises to stay in touch until then.

Marie doubled checked that the connection had been properly ended, just as Lizzy gushed.

"Is this guy totally likeable, or what?"

Kelly swiveled in her chair, "The feeling is completely different with him than with Manuel. Probably because we know their story, and it makes sense that he would be her second chance, just like she would be for him."

"I hope she doesn't have a bad reaction to us picking a boyfriend for her," Marie cautioned.

"We're not really picking him, we're just bringing him back into the picture," Lizzy countered, and in a voice full of laughter, she added, "since she thinks he's dead and all, we'll say we found him roaming with my see-through people with nothing better to do."

Kelly laughed but rejoined with a shrug to address Marie's concern, "If she doesn't like Alonzo as much as she likes Manuel, there is no doubt that she will cut him loose."

Marie again pointed out the obvious, "How are we going to keep this secret from her for the next three months?"

At the prospect, the sisters' silvery laughter rang in the room, "Indeed!"

Downstairs, Maggie stirred but did not wake. Angelo hugged her tight and kissed her goodbye.

Chapter 48

The series of first holidays—Christmas, New Year's, Valentines—leading up to Maggie's birthday, made it impossible to define, much less, award a prize for 'most euphoric' among the four women.

To anyone who would listen, Maggie rhapsodized about the symbolism of seventy-seven. "I'm in direct alignment with my soul's higher purpose, the angels say so."

Kelly, Lizzy, and Marie, having to guard the secret of their mother's birthday surprise, were in a heightened state of excitement that, as the date approached, drove them to avoid Maggie, for fear of giving it away.

The stress intensified when Alonzo arrived—the girls had booked him in a hotel only five minutes from the motherhouse—surely Maggie could sense the massive disturbance in energy fields!

On the day of, they arrived early at the venue, in varying degrees of anxiety.

Maggie pretended to listen but was so tense that she could not focus on anything anyone said to her. The girls, glad to release their own nervous energy, busied themselves with last minute details, before guests arrived.

And arrive they did.

"Promise to tell me when I need to touch up my lipstick," Maggie breathed, just as the receiving line began.

Kelly, who had her arm hooked to Maggie's, whispered back, "You bet."

From their mother's other side, Marie confessed to Lizzy, "My heart is beating so fast!"

"Mine's at the top of my throat—I'm trying not to choke on it."

Grandchildren, sisters, nieces, nephews, and the handful of friends Maggie had made in the short months since her arrival, all lined up to be hugged and kissed by her, and she graciously accepted all their birthday wishes.

After greeting over fifty people, and before she escorted Maggie to the main table, Kelly produced the promised lipstick.

The oldies playlist in the background, put together by her grandchildren to encapsulate Maggie's adult life, did what it was supposed to, and triggered lively conversations throughout the hall. Meanwhile, waiters floated about, pouring water, and setting bread baskets on each table.

Marie's husband, who had been entrusted to bring Alonzo to the party, knew to wait until all the guests were seated, so that an announcement could be made.

The moment was at hand.

Marie stood up abruptly and left the room, making a beeline for the ladies' room. Alarmed, Kelly and Lizzy followed her.

"Oh my God, what if we made a terrible mistake!" Marie hissed, on the verge of tears.

"What?"

"She's going to hate being put on the spot like this! What were we thinking?

Marie's sense of foreboding seemed to infect Lizzy as well, "Should we call and tell him not to come?"

Kelly gave Marie a one-armed hug, "No-no, it'll be OK. I know it will. The theme of the party is a trip down memory lane, and that's a perfect excuse. She won't take it as matchmaking effort, she'll take it for what it is. A chance to reconnect with an old friend, whose story she is now at liberty to explore."

"OK, you're right," Marie took a couple of deep breaths, "let's get out there."

"And face the music," Lizzy winked.

From a podium in the center of the banquet room, oldest to youngest, Maggie's daughters addressed their guests.

"First things first," Kelly flashed her dimpled smile, "thank you all so much for being here today, to help us celebrate this wonderful lady I get to call my mother."

"She has been our rock and our support. We may have stubbed our toes, over and over, on that rock," Lizzy teased, "but her constancy has seen us through our troubles. We are forever grateful for that."

Although she still looked a little shaken, Marie's voice was steady when she said, "Our mother shaped our lives with her example—she taught us how to throw proper parties, like this one," she paused for the ripple of laughter from the audience to subside. "But that is not all. As the birthday girl herself says, she is a lady who is in alignment with a higher purpose. Her whole life has followed a cosmic path full of sacrifices and blessings."

"Over the years, she learned to color the sacrifices life asked of her, with the vivid palette of her blessings, bringing home to us that attitude is everything," Lizzy declared.

"This is a woman of faith, who never lost sight of what mattered to her. And what matters to her, above all, is family," Kelly's glance roved over the happy faces in the room, "looking out, at all of you here, we see that our mother is clearly reaping what she sowed."

Doubts forgotten; Marie picked up the thread, "The pleasure of your company is all she asked for today, and already in this room are represented seven decades and seven years' worth of people in her life..."

"Knowing her love of surprises, we wanted to add one more on this special day..."

On hearing Lizzy's last, a collective, 'ooooh', rose from the tables and Maggie, who had been listening to her daughters with a knot in her throat, realized something unexpected was about to happen.

Marie continued where Lizzy left off.

"We are so happy the timing worked out, so that we could have a special guest here today. More than a guest, really, he is a visitor, come to us from 1961."

People whirled in their chairs, craned their necks toward the entryway, but Maggie clutched her heart, refusing to look. *From 1961?*

Two men were coming toward her—*Marie's husband, yes, but who is*—

"Mom," Kelly had come from the podium. Lizzy, and Marie too, had appeared beside her, "say hello to Alonzo."

Maggie's eyes swiveled from one smiling face to the other, unable to comprehend, "It can't be!"

"Go on! He's come all this way to see you," Marie said, kissing her cheek.

Maggie stood up on wobbly legs.

"I think we got you good!" Lizzy giggled. Maggie steadied herself enough to pinch her daughter's arm, "Ouch!"

"Oh, my goodness! I don't believe it! How can this be?"

"Happy Birthday, Maggie," Alonzo beamed.

Everyone's excited chatter, as the girls helped spread the explanation from table to table, drowned out the rest of their exchange.

A few minutes later, Lizzy elbowed Kelly and jutted her chin toward the main table, "Look."

Alonzo gallantly pulled the chair out for Maggie. She sat down, and he took the seat next to her, taking advantage of the unexpected privacy granted to them by the cheerful, crowded room.

"Well, we've lost the birthday girl," Kelly laughed, "she better tell us every last word he said!"

"With any luck, she'll break away to at least blow out her own candles," Marie teased.

Four hours later, as the sound of clinking glasses and silverware on dishes started to die down, the girls raised their glasses, congratulating themselves in hushed voices over the successful operation; they had pulled off reuniting their mother with her fiancé from fifty years ago!

"Do we want to bet on how long before we're hosting another big party, as daughters of the bride?" Lizzy smirked.

Shaking with laughter, Kelly put in, "I don't know, she'll want to be properly courted, you know how she is."

Marie raised her glass to her sisters, "My money is on three years from now, for her eightieth."

"She has such a cool energy about her," Kelly said, feasting on the sight of a radiant Maggie, "I swear she doesn't look like she is seventy-seven-years old."

"The angels do seem to conspire to make her happy, and give her everything she wants," Marie reflected.

"Hmmm, angels and stars can conspire all they want," Lizzy countered, "I think the bigger deal is that she makes up her mind about what she has, and decides that happiness is wanting exactly that."

As if plucking their conversation from the air, Maggie broke from the newly familiar spell of Alonzo's voice, and directed a summoning glance at her daughters.

They turned to her in unison, holding glasses aloft and blowing kisses.

Maggie shook a fist at them, but the dazzling smile that followed, left no doubt that her birthday surprise was exactly as she would have it.

The End

A Word from Editorial Reviewers and Beta-Readers

"*Love & Homegrown Magic* is beautifully written, mystical and very energizing. Kept me engaged. Truly a love story. I could relate with the culture of the plot since I was brought up catholic and still believe in the power of angels. Great book. Wishing you much success."
—*Adela Hofmann*

"The characters come alive and pull you into their lives. Ms. Bossano paints a vivid portrait that will not let you put it down."
—*Brian Peters*

"*Love & Homegrown Magic* is a magical story with all the twists and turns that make for a very enjoyable read. I couldn't put the book down because the characters were so likable and well developed. I became so interested in the lives of Maggie and her three daughters that the story flew by. Patricia Bossano has a unique style of writing that is so enjoyable. I can't wait to read her next book."
—*Kirk Raeber, author*

"This book made me remember my childhood since I have similar experiences to Maggie's life. The personal growth of the characters was just on point."
—*Magdalena Lozano*

"*Love & Homegrown Magic* was so easy to read! The story flows so well and the author paints a clear picture for readers to delve into for as many hours as they choose. Be warned, it will take a few minutes to get back to reality after you've been in the book for a bit."

—*Paul Wold*

"Thank you for writing this story! Having worked on breaking familial patterns and healing ancestral pains, it's lovely to see it laid out in such a simple way. I often find it becomes a rather tangled ball of different colored threads one needs to pick apart in order to weave them together into a whole that makes sense. I also love how easily you brought Maggie's beliefs together to form something that surpasses religion to become faith."

—*Yanieke Terband, Alchemy*

"I've thought about how to describe "Love & Homegrown Magic" in one word, and the word I keep coming back to is *celestial*. If this is how you would like the book to seem, then I must commend you because it has some of the strongest writing I have seen for a while."

—*Maggie, Beta-Reader*

"I genuinely enjoyed the way "Love & Homegrown Magic" pulled me through a beautiful variety of emotions. Maggie is very relatable as a mother and the sisterhood feels so real. Reading the novel was more than enjoyable, I found myself intrigued and wanting to know what would happen next. The hardships that the author included were excellently represented through her words and the world she built with them. It was a new take to watch a character change and grow since birth and I think that aids in my connection with Maggie as a reader."

—*Jessica, Beta-Reader*

Patricia Bossano

is the author of award-winning philosophical fantasy novels and supernatural escapes. She lives and writes in California with her family.

I would love to hear your thoughts!

If you enjoyed *Love & Homegrown Magic*,
please let me know at: author@patriciabossano.com.
A review at the outlet of your choice would be
greatly appreciated too.

CPSIA information can be obtained
at www.ICGtesting.com
Printed in the USA
LVHW030433231020
669603LV00021B/412/J

9 781732 509337